AN ADAPTED CLASSIC

Lord Jim

Joseph Conrad

Globe
Fearon

Upper Saddle River, New Jersey
www.globefearon.com

Adapter: William Caper
Project Editor: David Cutts
Lead Editors: Kathy Bentzen and Meredith Diskin
Production Editor: Marcela Maslanczuk
Marketing Manager: Kate Krimsky
Art Supervision: Angel Weyant, Eileen Peters
Art Coordinator: Cindy Talocci
Electronic Page Production: Leslie Greenberg,
Susan Levine, Wanda Rockwell
Manufacturing Supervisor: Mark Cirillo
Cover and Interior Illustrator: Janet Wilson

Printed in the United States of America
1 2 3 4 5 6 7 8 9 10   04 03 02 01 00

ISBN: 0-130-23697-7

Globe
Fearon

1-800-848-9500
www.globefearon.com

CONTENTS

ABOUT THE AUTHOR

Joseph Conrad was born Józef Teodor Konrad Korzeniowski in the Polish Ukraine, on December 3, 1857. This region had been part of Poland, but in 1857 it was under the control of Russia. Conrad's parents, accused of plotting against Russian authorities, were arrested and sent to northern Russia. Conrad, who was four years old, went with them. When Conrad's mother died, his father sent their seven-year-old son back to Poland to live with his uncle. Conrad never saw his father again. His father died when Conrad was 11 years old.

When he was 16, Conrad went to France and began working on French ships. In 1878, he joined the British Merchant Navy. By the time he was 29, Conrad spoke three languages—Polish, French, and English.

Conrad became a second mate, a first mate, and finally a ship's captain. He traveled all over the world and made many voyages to Asia, where *Lord Jim* is set. It was on these long sea voyages that he began to write.

In 1886, Conrad became a British citizen. That same year, he wrote his first short story. In 1895, Conrad gave up his life at sea, married, and became a full-time writer. His first novel, which he had started while at sea, was published that same year. *Lord Jim*, his twelfth book, was published in 1900.

Conrad's books were highly praised by critics, but they did not sell well. He was writing novels in a new way, and people often found his books difficult to understand. When he wrote *Lord Jim*, Conrad was poor and unhappy.

In 1914, when his novel *Chance* became a best seller in Britain and the United States, Conrad finally found success as a writer. People all over the world began reading his books.

Conrad died in August 1924. Today, he is considered one of the world's great writers, and *Lord Jim* is regarded as a literary masterpiece.

ADAPTER'S NOTE

In preparing this edition of *Lord Jim*, we have kept as close as possible to Joseph Conrad's original words and style. We have changed some of the vocabulary. We have also shortened and combined some chapters. Some of the footnotes explain difficult words. Other footnotes fill in historical details.

PREFACE

Conrad wrote *Lord Jim* during the years 1898–1900. Originally, it was going to be a short story. However, as Conrad worked on his story, it grew into a novel.

When *Lord Jim* first appeared, it confused readers. People were used to novels that took them from one event to another in a way that was easy to follow. *Lord Jim*, however, moves back and forth in time and has more than one narrator.

In the first two chapters, the story is told by an unnamed narrator. In Chapter 3, a character named Marlow takes over as narrator and tells most of the tale.

Most of the time, Conrad has Marlow tell the reader about his direct experiences with Jim. At other times, he has Marlow relate what others have told him about Jim.

The story also skips around in time. While one event is being described, Conrad has Marlow suddenly move back in time to talk about something that happened weeks, months, or even years before. Sometimes Conrad has Marlow move *forward* in time and has him describe an event that will happen later in the story. When Marlow does this, he often gives the reader only a hint about this future event. He does not reveal exactly what happens until later.

Conrad believed that there is no one right way to look at events. As *Lord Jim* unfolds, the reader is presented with different views about who Jim is and why he does what he does. This leaves the reader to decide if Jim's actions are right or wrong. That is exactly what Conrad intended.

HISTORICAL BACKGROUND

The main events in *Lord Jim* take place between 1883 and 1889. At this time, the British Empire was at the height of its power. England had colonies all around the world, which lead to the saying, "the sun never sets on the British Empire."

Other European countries also had colonies. It was a common belief in Europe that Europeans were a more advanced people, with a duty to help the "backward" people in other parts of the world. Most of the citizens of countries that had colonies thought that they were superior to the people of their colonies. It was not unusual for the native people of these colonies to sometimes believe this, too. For example, when Conrad's characters Jim and Brown come to Patusan from the "outside world," the people in Patusan are immediately afraid of them. They are cautious about how they deal with these outsiders.

When new characters are introduced, Marlow often tells which country they come from. At the time *Lord Jim* takes place, this information was important because it influenced how the characters would be treated.

Conrad traveled all over the world and made many voyages to Asian cities. These are the Eastern ports referred to in *Lord Jim*. However, Conrad never tells us exactly where the story takes place. He based Lord Jim on stories he heard and people he met in his travels, but the story itself is fictional. By not relating exactly where these events happen, Conrad is stating that they could happen to anyone in any part of the world.

MAJOR CHARACTERS

Jim (Tuan Jim or Lord Jim) An English ship's officer; the main character of the book

Marlow An English ship's captain who helps Jim; the main narrator of Jim's story

Stein A rich merchant who sends Jim to Patusan

Doramin The powerful leader of the tribe called the Bugis

Rajah Allang A powerful leader in Patusan; Jim's enemy

Sherif Ali A third powerful leader in Patusan trying to take over the Bugis villiage

Jewel The woman whom Jim falls in love with

Dain Waris Jim's friend; the son of Doramin

Tamb' Itam Jim's loyal servant in Patusan

Cornelius Jewel's stepfather

Brown A pirate who invades Patusan

Chapter 1

He was almost six feet tall, perhaps two inches less. He was powerfully built. His shoulders stooped slightly, and as he walked toward you, with his head forward and a fixed stare, he looked like a charging bull. His voice was deep and loud. He was confident but never forced himself on people. He was extremely neat and was dressed in white from shoes to hat. He was popular in all the Eastern ports where he worked as a water-clerk for a ship chandler.[1]

A good water-clerk greets the captains of arriving ships before the other water-clerks. He makes sure the captain visits his store to buy the ship's supplies. Chandlers sell everything a ship needs, from chains and paint to food and wine. The water-clerk visits the ship every day while it's in the harbor and treats the captain as if he's an old friend. The happier the captain is, the more supplies he will buy.

Good water-clerks are hard to find, and those who also know the sea are especially rare. So Jim was always paid well, and his employers tried very hard to keep him satisfied. Even so, he would suddenly quit his job and disappear. As much as his employers liked him, after he left they called him a fool.

To the people who met him, he was just Jim. Of course, he had another name, but he didn't want anyone to know it. He was mysterious because he had a secret. Whenever the secret was revealed, he would quickly leave the seaport where he happened to be and go on to another one. He always moved east, and he lived in seaports because he was still a sailor, a sailor in exile[2] from the sea. No matter where he went, his secret followed him. For many years, he was

---

1. ship chandler a person who sells supplies to ships
2. in exile absent, or removed

known simply as Jim the water-clerk. Later, when he finally went to live in the jungle of Malaya, the people there added another word to his name. They called him Tuan[3] Jim, which meant Lord Jim.

Jim grew up in England,[4] where his father was a minister. When he decided he wanted to go to sea, he was sent to a training ship for officers. The men on the ship liked him. His usual post was on a platform at the top of the ship's front mast. From there, he looked down at the world and at all the ships in the harbor. He imagined a life full of adventure and bravery.

He saw himself saving people from sinking ships, or helping to stop a ship from crashing into rocks. He imagined himself alone on a deserted island or in a tiny boat showing his comrades how to be brave after their ship had sunk.

One winter's day, there was a terrible storm on the river where his training ship was anchored. A boat trying to escape the storm crashed into another boat. The men on the training ship were rushing to help, and Jim ran up on deck. There, he stopped and stood still in awe of the storm. The air was full of flying water, and the wind howled. The Earth and sky were raging, and it all seemed to be directed at him. People bumped and pushed him as they ran by. He caught hold of a rope as he staggered against a mast.

As he stood there, his shipmates lowered a small rescue boat. He rushed forward to get into the boat, but he heard a splash as it dropped into the sea.

Jim was about to leap overboard and join the men in the rescue boat when he felt his shoulder gripped firmly. "Too late," his captain told him. Jim turned to the captain with a look of defeat. The captain smiled and said, "Better luck next time. This will teach you to be fast."

---

3. **Tuan** pronounced: twahn
4. Here the author begins a flashback in which the reader learns about Jim's background.

The men from his ship saved two people that day. However, when Jim thought about it later, the storm seemed to be very small and not dangerous at all. He realized that there was no reason to be in awe of it. Some day he would face things that were far more dangerous, and he would face them better than anyone else.

That night, while the others traded excited stories about the rescue, Jim stayed by himself. He felt they were bragging. He thought their feelings of being brave were as false as his fear had been. He was also angry with the storm for catching him when he was not ready.

Looking back on what had happened, he was glad he had not gotten into the rescue boat. Far bigger and braver things were in store for him. He had learned a great deal just by watching the others. From now on, he would know how to deal with a storm at sea. He was sure, more than ever, that he would lead a life of adventure and courage.

After two years of training he went to sea. He was finally able to visit the places he had been dreaming about for so long. Even though he made many voyages, he found little adventure.

Life at sea is a lot of hard work day after day. Yet, Jim wanted no other life because he loved being on the sea. His future looked good. In time, when he was still very young, he became chief mate[5] of a good ship— even though he had never been tested in an emergency.

During this time, Jim saw the deadly fury of the sea only once. During a storm, he was hit and badly injured by a falling pole. The storm lasted for a week, and because Jim was injured, he had to stay in his cabin. As the ship tossed and rolled on the angry sea, Jim lay in his bed and could only imagine what dangers awaited anyone up on deck. Secretly, he was

---

5. **chief mate** an officer just below captain in rank

glad he did not have to go up there. When the storm was over and the sea was calm again, he thought no more about such things.

When his ship arrived at an eastern port, Jim was sent to a hospital. It took him a long time to heal, and his ship sailed on without him.

When he could walk again, he started looking for a job on a ship that would take him home. However, there were no jobs available. After a while he gave up the idea of going home, and he signed on as chief mate of a ship named the *Patna*.

The *Patna* was a local steamer, as old as the hills and as rusty as an old water tank. Its captain was a German who spoke badly of his country and bullied people. On this voyage, the *Patna* was carrying 800 pilgrims on a religious journey.

Families, young and old men, shy little girls, and timid women all came aboard the *Patna* in silence. Poor people from all over Asia were making this voyage as an expression of their religious faith. They were covered with dust and dressed in rags. The German captain called them cattle.

When everyone was on board, the *Patna* began its voyage. The sky was clear, the sun was hot, and the sea was so calm that there was barely a ripple in the water.

As the *Patna* steamed across the ocean, it spread a ribbon of black smoke across the sky and left a ribbon of white foam on the water. As if left by a ghost, the foam disappeared immediately.

Each day, the sun blazed down on the *Patna* and on the people aboard it. To protect themselves from the fierce heat, the pilgrims huddled under canvas tents that were put up on the deck. It was so hot that they stayed under the tents all day. The *Patna's* crew might have forgotten they were there if not for the low murmur of their sad voices. Day after day, the sun struck the ship like a blast shot from the sky. When night finally came and darkness fell, it was like a blessing.

Chapter 2

The night was wonderfully still. Stars gleamed with a soft light that made the world feel very safe. The moon was like a thin piece of gold, and the sea was as smooth as a sheet of ice.

At his post on the *Patna*, Jim felt safe and at peace. Under the tents on the deck, the pilgrims were sleeping on mats, blankets, and bare planks. They were wrapped in colorful cloths and rags, and their heads rested on small bundles. They took up every bit of space on and below deck.

Two Malays[6] were silently steering the *Patna*, one on either side of her big brass wheel. Jim's footsteps sounded loud in the quiet night, as if they were echoed by the stars. His eyes roamed the horizon, seeming to gaze into the unknown, but they did not see what was about to happen. The only shadow on the sea was the shadow of the black smoke from the ship's smokestack.

Jim glanced at the ship's compass. He looked at the chart of the ship's course. Everything was fine, and he felt very good.

"How steady the ship goes," he thought with wonder. He liked how peaceful the sea and sky were. At times like this, his thoughts were full of brave deeds. He loved these dreams and the success that he imagined. They were the best part of life. In these dreams, he could face anything. He sighed happily and was a little sorry that soon he would have to go down to his cabin to sleep.

---

6. Malays people from the country of Malaya

The captain had silently come on deck. He was wearing his pajamas, his face was red, and he was still half asleep. He looked at the chart and scratched his ribs. Jim treated the captain with respect, but he thought the man was disgusting.

"It's too hot below decks," said a voice. It was the *Patna's* second engineer. The captain ignored him, and the engineer kept complaining. Finally, the captain growled, "Shut up."

The engineer was drunk, which made the captain very angry. They began to argue, and now Jim was glad he would be going down to his cabin in ten minutes. These men did not belong to the world of great adventure. Jim worked with them, but he was not like them. He was different.

The second engineer swore that he was not drunk. Then, he said he was not afraid of anything the captain could do to him, and he was not afraid of anything else. "I don't know what fear is," he claimed, and he went on and on about how brave he was. As he spoke, he waved his arms and walked back and forth.

Suddenly, he fell down on his face as if he had been hit from behind with a club. Jim and the captain stepped forward to help him, but then they stopped and looked at the sea. It was still completely calm.

What had happened? Why did the second engineer fall? Suddenly, the calm sea and the cloudless sky did not seem safe at all. Something terrible seemed about to happen.

The second engineer got up, only to fall down again. "What's that?" he said. There was a low sound like distant thunder. Then, a tiny vibration could be felt in the ship, as if the *Patna* quivered in response to the thunder, and the thunder was deep in the water. The two Malays who were steering the ship glanced at the captain, but their hands remained on the ship's wheel.

The ship rose a few inches in the water, then settled down and continued across the calm sea. Its quivering stopped, and the faint noise of thunder disappeared. It was as though the ship had steamed across a narrow belt of vibrating water and humming air.

Weeks later, at the trial, when Jim tried to describe what happened, he said, "The ship went over whatever it was as easily as a snake crawling over a stick."

As he sat in the witness box, looking out at all those staring faces, the crowded courtroom was very quiet. His own voice rang in his ears. Jim was asked, "After you decided you had crashed into something floating in the water, you were ordered by your captain to see if there was any damage. Did you think there was damage to your ship?"

"I did not," Jim answered. "I was told to tell no one on the ship. We didn't want to create a panic. I took a lantern and opened a hatch in the deck. I heard splashing below. I looked down and saw that an area in the front of the ship was more than half filled with water. I knew there must be a big hole in the ship. There was only one bulkhead[7] between this area and another part of the ship that was filled with people. I went back to tell the captain.

"When I saw the second engineer again, he seemed dazed. He told me he thought his left arm was broken. While I was in the front of the ship, he had fallen down a ladder. When I told him what I had seen, he exclaimed, 'That rotten bulkhead will give way in a minute, and the ship will go down like a lump of lead!' He pushed me away with his good arm and ran up a ladder shouting. The engineer ran toward the engine room."

Jim spoke slowly as he answered questions at the trial because he wanted to make them understand

---

7. bulkhead a wall in a ship

exactly what had happened. However, he didn't think they would. To understand, they had to be there, and none of the people who were asking him all of those questions had been on the *Patna* that night.

As Jim answered their questions, he looked around at the people in the big room. He noticed a man who sat apart from the others. The man's face was tired and worried, and he had quiet eyes that were honest and clear. This man did not look at Jim with the same stare as the others in the room. Jim thought, "He's looking at me as if he can see somebody or something past my shoulder."

Jim continued to answer all of the questions about what happened, but he was sure his answers did not matter. He thought that even speaking the truth was not going to help. The man who was looking at him seemed to understand this. Then, the man turned away.

After the trial, that man, a sea captain whose name was Marlow, remembered Jim well. He would tell Jim's story often. He usually told the story after dinner as he and his guests relaxed on a porch and smoked cigars. With his first word, Marlow would become very still— as if he had traveled back through time and was speaking to his listeners from the past.

Chapter 3

Marlow would say,[8] "Oh yes, I attended the trial. To this day I wonder why I went. Maybe I was supposed to look out for Jim and protect him if I could. Maybe I'm the kind of man people like to tell their secrets to. Maybe I just like to be able to tell stories after dinner.

---

8. At this point, Marlow becomes the narrator and tells Jim's story.

"My eyes first met Jim's eyes at the trial. The big room was crowded, because by the time the trial started, everyone knew about the incident. It was all people talked about.

"I even saw the men from the *Patna* before the trial. One morning, I was standing outside the harbor office when I saw four men walking toward me. I knew immediately that it was them. The captain of the *Patna* was the fattest man in the Tropics.[9] He made me think of a trained baby elephant walking on its back legs. He was walking very fast and went into the harbor office to give his report.

"The harbor master yelled at him so loudly that I could hear it in the street. In a few minutes, he came out of the harbor office and stood a few feet away from me shaking and swearing.

"The three men who were with him stayed at a distance and waited for him. One of these men had his arm in a sling. One of them was very thin. The other was a tall, handsome young man. He stood with his back to the others and stared at the sky. This was the very first time I saw Jim. He looked as if he didn't have a care in the world. I was amazed, and a little angry, that he was so calm. I thought that, if someone like him can go wrong, what hope is there for the rest of us?

" 'The harbor master called me a hound,' the captain of the *Patna* said to me. 'I don't care! The Pacific Ocean is big! There's plenty of room for a man like me. You Englishmen are no better than other people! That harbor master thinks he has the right to yell at me just because he is English!' Now, the captain was shaking. 'Take away my certificate![10] Take it! I don't want it. I spit on it!' He spat.

---

9. the Tropics the region near the Equator
10. certificate The captain is referring to the official paper that says he is a trained ship's officer. Without a certificate, he would not be hired to work on a good ship.

"I was curious about how all this was affecting the young fellow. However, when I glanced at Jim, I saw that it didn't seem to affect him at all. He stood with his hands in his pockets and his back to the captain. He looked as if he were waiting for a friend so they could go for a walk together.

"I was surprised. I expected to see him scared, confused, and squirming. After all, there's nothing more awful than getting caught. I don't mean getting caught breaking the law. I mean getting caught revealing your greatest weakness.

"It takes strength to be honest, but that sort of strength is common. It's easy to have. Still, who has strength when it comes to facing our greatest weakness? We may not even know we have a weakness—until we need a special strength that we just don't have. Jim had been caught.

"Therefore, when I saw him standing there, apparently without a care in the world, I was surprised. However, I also liked him immediately. I could tell he was one of us. He was a gentleman. He knew the importance of facing life with courage and being a decent man.

"He was the kind of fellow I would leave in charge of a ship. I ought to know. I've been a ship's captain for many years. I would have trusted my ship to that young man just by looking at him. Yet, it wouldn't have been a safe thing to do.

"That shows how much I would have trusted Jim from his appearance alone. You see, he looked as though he was perfect, but he had a flaw.[11] I was more interested in this flaw than in any crime of which he was accused.

"The two men standing near Jim walked over to their captain. The captain opened his mouth to

---

11. flaw something that keeps a person or thing from being perfect speak, but he said nothing. Instead, he turned and walked away.

"He went to a carriage[12] that was waiting nearby and climbed in. The carriage shook and rocked under his weight, and I expected it to turn over. The captain ordered the driver to leave and off he went, leaving the two men standing there with their mouths hanging open in surprise. No one ever saw him again.

"The day before the trial started, I went to the hospital to visit one of my men. Those two men from the *Patna* were there.

"The second engineer, the man with the broken arm, was light-headed with fever. The other man, the chief engineer, had been brought in extremely drunk.

"The chief engineer grabbed my shoulder and spoke in a loud voice. 'Only *my* eyes were good enough to see. I am famous for my eyesight! You don't believe me? Look under the bed!'

"He was so upset that I looked under his bed. Of course I saw nothing, and I told him so.

"Downstairs, I saw a doctor. He told me that the first engineer was having visions from drinking too much. 'He won't be able to go to the trial,' the doctor told me. 'Do you think his evidence is important?'

"'Not in the least,' I answered.

"The authorities seemed to agree. The trial took place on schedule. The courtroom was full. Jim was the only one of the *Patna's* officers who was able and willing to stand trial.

"By now, everyone knew about it. It was impossible to find out exactly how the *Patna* was damaged, but no one cared about that anyway. People came to the trial because they were curious to see Jim. They wanted to know what kind of person he was. However, the trial would not tell them that. He was asked

---

12. carriage a horse-drawn vehicle

questions that would tell *what* happened but wouldn't explain *why* it happened.

"One of the men who had been picked to be a judge for this case was a ship's captain named Brierly. He was the captain of an excellent ship, and he had never made a mistake or had an accident. He never doubted his ability to do the right thing. He had saved lives at sea and had rescued ships in danger. He thought he had the best ship on the sea and that he was the best captain.

"A week after the trial, Captain Brierly killed himself by jumping off of his ship and letting himself drown. He planned it very carefully. He even chose the exact spot where he would jump. Once he jumped, he didn't swim a stroke to save himself.

"Why did he do it? I think that while he was sitting in judgment on Jim at the trial, he was secretly thinking about himself. He was judging himself. He must have found himself guilty.

"We'll never know why Brierly killed himself. Perhaps he thought that if he were in the same position Jim was in, he might have done what Jim did. Perhaps he didn't want to live in a world where honor is so important.

"I happened to speak with Captain Brierly on the first day of the trial. He came up to me in the street. I was surprised to see that he was upset, because he always appeared so calm.

"'Why bother with this trial?' he said to me. 'It's stupid.' Then, he grabbed me by the coat. 'Why are we tormenting that young man?'

"'I don't know,' I answered. 'Maybe because he lets you do it.'

"'Can't he see that his captain has run away?' Brierly asked. 'What does he expect to happen? Nothing can save him. Why does he sit there and take it?'

"We walked in silence for a few steps, and I wondered why Brierly was having these thoughts. Now, I believe he was thinking about himself. I said that maybe Jim didn't have the money to run away.

"'Well then,' Brierly responded, 'let him creep 20 feet under the ground and stay there! That's what *I* would do!'

"I suggested that Jim was showing courage by staying and facing things.

"'I don't care about that kind of courage!' Brierly said. 'I'll give him some money if you'll make him leave town tomorrow morning. He's a gentleman. He'll understand. He must! He's making all of us look bad! If he went away this would all stop.'

"Brierly stopped speaking for a moment. Then, he said, "Talk to him, Marlow. I can't do it because of my position, but you can do it.'

"I refused to interfere. I decided that, for Jim, the trial was a great punishment in itself. For him, not running away showed that he was not a bad person. Brierly was angry when he walked away from me.

"I was at the trial the next day. I watched both Brierly and Jim. It was on that day, while I was looking at Jim, that our eyes met. The look on his face discouraged any plan I might have had to speak to him. I felt I couldn't help him.

"Soon after our eyes met, the trial stopped for the day. As I walked out with the crowd, I saw Jim standing in the hall with his back to everyone. Just as we passed Jim, the man walking next to me stumbled over a yellow dog that someone had brought into the hall.

"The man laughed and said, 'Look at that miserable dog.' As soon as he said this, he and I were separated by the crowd.

"Suddenly Jim spun around, walked toward me, and blocked my path. As he glared at me, I almost felt as if I was being held up by a bandit.

" 'Did you speak to me?' he asked, very low, as he leaned close to me.

"I said, 'No.' Something in the sound of his voice warned me to be very careful.

" 'I heard you,' he said. Looking at his face was like looking at the sky before a huge storm. Yet, he wasn't threatening me. In fact, he was very quiet.

" 'I won't let any man call me names outside of this court,' he said.

"I didn't know what he was talking about, and I didn't know what to do. We stared at each other. Then, he took a step toward me. I thought I would have no choice but to fight him.

" 'Will you kindly tell me what I've said or done?' I asked.

" 'Who's a dog?' he demanded. Then, at last, I understood.

" 'No one called you a dog. This is all a big mistake.' I pointed to the dog, which was still in the hall. Jim stared at it as if he had never seen a dog before. 'Nobody dreamed of insulting you,' I said.

"He was so embarrassed that he turned bright red, and his lips trembled as if he might cry. He couldn't even talk. He made a strange noise in his throat as if he had been struck on the head. It made me feel very bad to see him like this. He had been caught again.

"He turned and walked away very quickly. I had to run to catch up with him. When I asked him why he was running away, he said, 'Never! I run from no one on Earth.'

"We walked together for a while, and I told him I didn't want him thinking that I had meant to insult him. He said it was his mistake and asked me to understand. With people staring at him in court all day, he expected someone to insult him.

" 'I can't let that happen,' he told me. 'In court, it's different. I have to take that—and I can do it.'

"I don't pretend I understood him. The views he let me have of him were like glimpses through a thick fog."

Chapter 4

"I invited Jim to have dinner with me at my hotel, and he accepted my invitation.

"Jim began to talk to me freely. He seemed to have completely forgotten our awkward conversation outside of the court. I liked him. He was a decent man. He was one of us—a gentleman.

He talked with either self-control or deceit. Who can tell.

"I said that the trial must be awfully hard for him. He threw his arm across the table, grabbed my hand, and stared at me. 'It is hell,' he said softly.

"We went to another room for coffee. 'I couldn't run away from the trial,' Jim began. 'The captain did, but I couldn't, and I wouldn't. The others from the *Patna* have gotten out of the trial in one way or another, but I wouldn't try.'

"I listened carefully. He began by saying that he could never go home. 'My father has read all about it in the newspapers by now. I couldn't face him,' he told me. Then, he added, 'He wouldn't understand.'

"It was important to him, he told me, that I didn't think he was like the other men from the *Patna*.

He was not one of them. He was a different kind of person. I didn't argue with him. Then, he began to wonder what he would do after the trial was over. He would have no certificate, no career, and no money.

"He rose from his chair, went to the window, and looked out into the night. Then, he came back and stood towering above me. 'Do you know what *you* would have done if you had been on the *Patna?*' he asked.

"What a question! Before I could respond, he went on, 'It's all in being ready. I wasn't ready—not then. I don't want to make excuses for myself, but I would like to explain. I would like somebody to understand. One person at least! You! Why not you?'

"He quietly began to tell me his story. Jim explained that he and the other three men from the *Patna* had been picked up at sea by a ship called the *Avondale.* The *Patna's* captain told the men on the *Avondale* a story he had made up, and at first, they believed him. The men from the *Patna* spent ten days aboard the *Avondale.* I didn't ask Jim how he felt then. He told me nothing about how he felt when the *Avondale* reached port and they learned the truth about what had happened to the *Patna.*

" 'That bulkhead held after all,' I said.

" 'Yes,' he murmured, 'it held. Yet, I swear I felt it bulge under my hand.'

" 'It's amazing how much old iron can take sometimes,' I pointed out.

"He slapped his thigh. 'Ah! What a chance missed! What a chance missed!' he cried out as if he were in pain. Then, he fell silent again as he thought about his missed opportunity.

"I brought him back to earth by saying, 'You mean, you missed your chance to stay with the ship.'

"He looked at me with his eyes suddenly full of pain and his face bewildered. It was as though he had tumbled down from a star. I don't think that any of us will ever look like *that*. He shuddered as if a cold finger had touched his heart. Then, he sighed.

"'The bulkhead bulged!' he repeated. 'A piece of rust as big as the palm of my hand fell off of it. It was starting to come apart. Do you think I was thinking of myself? There were 160 people sleeping in the section of the ship next to the bulkhead and more people sleeping on the deck! Even if there was time to warn them, there were three times as many people as there were lifeboats for! I expected to see the bulkhead burst as I stood there! What could I do?'

"He went on to tell me that his first thought was to shout and wake everyone up. However, he felt so helpless that he could not make a sound. Therefore, he ran back to the deck. He admitted that his knees were shaking as he stood on the deck. The ship's engines had stopped and the escaping steam was hissing loudly. It made a deep rumble that caused the ship to tremble.

"The deck was crowded with people. Most of them were sleeping, but every now and then someone would sit up and listen. Yet, no one took notice of the strange noise that the ship was making.

"He believed that the ship would go down at any moment, and he thought that all of the people would die. Nothing could save them! There was no time. No time! Therefore, it didn't make much sense to warn them—there would only be panic and everyone would die anyway.

"'I saw as clearly as I see you now,' he told me, 'that there was nothing I could do. I thought I might just as well stand where I was and wait. I thought the ship would go down in a matter of seconds.'

"Suddenly the steam stopped escaping from the engines, and it was very quiet. That made everything worse. 'I thought I would choke before I drowned,' he told me.

"He did not even think of saving himself. His only thought was that there were 800 people and only seven lifeboats. He didn't care if he was about to die. 'Somebody was speaking inside my head,' he said to me a little wildly. 'Eight hundred people—seven boats—and no time!'

"He leaned toward me across the table. 'Do you think I was afraid of death?' he asked in a fierce voice. He brought his hand down on the table with a bang. 'I swear I was not!'

"I realized that Jim wasn't afraid of death, but he was afraid of the emergency. He imagined all of the horrors of panic—the trampling rush, the horrible screams, and boats turned over in the water—and all of the terrible things that he had ever heard about a disaster at sea. He might have been ready to die, but I think he wanted to die without added terrors. He wanted to die quietly.

"I don't know how long he stood on that deck waiting to feel the ship go down under him. I'm sure it wasn't very long. Then, he got the idea of cutting the ropes holding the lifeboats. When the *Patna* sank, the lifeboats would float free.

"He started to run and stepped over the sleeping people. Suddenly, someone caught hold of his coat. In the light of his lantern, he saw that he had been grabbed by a passenger. The man kept saying the word 'water.' Jim pulled away, but the man grabbed his leg.

" 'He clung to me like a drowning man,' Jim said. "Water, water!" What did he mean? As calmly as I could, I ordered him to let go of me. He was stopping me, and there was very little time. Besides, other people were beginning to wake up. I wanted time to cut the lifeboats loose.

" 'The man followed me. He wouldn't keep quiet. He tried to shout, and I started to choke him. Then, I understood what he wanted. He wanted some drinking water. He had a young boy with him, and the boy was sick and thirsty. I dashed into my cabin, grabbed my water bottle, and I gave it to him. Then he vanished.

" 'I ran for the lifeboats. I saw the captain and three of the ship's engineers trying to get one of the boats ready. Then, I felt a heavy blow on my shoulder, just missing my head. The chief engineer was swinging a heavy rope at me. When he swung it again, I dodged out of the way. I lifted him off the deck as if he were a little child. He whispered, "Don't! Don't! I thought you were one of *them*."

" 'I shoved him to the side, and he crashed into the second engineer. Then, the captain came at me with his head down and growling like a wild beast. I stood where I was—as steady as a rock. I wasn't afraid of them. I drew my fist back and the captain stopped and muttered, "Ah! It's you. Quick, help us."

" 'Aren't you going to do something?' I asked.

" 'Yes. Clear out,' the captain snarled at me. At first, I didn't know what he meant. I saw that the ship was completely still in the water but slanting down a little. I thought about trying to shore up the bulkhead with boards, but I knew that no one would go down there with me. You think I'm a dog for doing nothing, but what would *you* have done? What good would it have been to make those people crazy with fear when I couldn't save them? No one could have saved them.'

"Listening to Jim's story, I felt as if I were being asked to understand things that were impossible to understand or to settle an argument that was impossible to settle. It was like trying to tell the difference between clear truth and lies that might have some truth in them. All of this made me very uncomfortable.

"He told his story very well. He sat there and told me that he wasn't afraid to face anything. Ever since he was a young boy, he'd been preparing himself for all the dangers that can happen on land and on water.

"'It is always the unexpected that happens,' I said.

"'I was caught when I wasn't ready,' he told me.

"Then, he continued telling me what happened on the *Patna*. As the captain and the engineers struggled to free the lifeboat, it stuck. They were working frantically to free it, but he didn't help them. He stood off to the side—as far from them as he could. Meanwhile, the two Malays who were steering the *Patna* stayed at their positions and held the ship's wheel.

"The chief engineer yelled at Jim to help them with the lifeboat, but he didn't move. Then, the engineer started to curse him, called him a coward, and even threatened to kill him.

"'Coward! He called me a coward!' Jim said to me. Then he threw himself back in his chair and shook with laughter. He laughed so loudly that the other guests in the dining room stared at him. He didn't care.

"When he finally stopped laughing, he said, 'By now I wanted the boat to sink. I wanted it to be over.'

"The captain and the engineers yelled and cursed as they struggled with the lifeboat. Then, the chief engineer pointed to the sea behind the *Patna*.

"Jim turned and saw a huge, dark storm approaching the ship. It blocked out a third of the sky. Storms like these appear suddenly and strike with immense fury. The wind, rain, and waves smash against everything in their path. When the storm came closer and its waves hit the *Patna*, the bulkhead would burst, and the ship would go straight to the bottom of the sea. The men struggling with the lifeboat became more frantic.

"It was then that Jim remembered that he wanted to cut the lifeboats free of the ship. He whipped out his knife and slashed at the ropes holding the lifeboats as if he hadn't seen the storm approaching. The others thought he was crazy.

"When he had cut all of the lifeboats loose, the chief engineer yelled at him, 'You're a fool! When those people are in the water, you won't have a chance. They'll smash your head from those boats!'

"Jim ignored him and the other men. He wouldn't even look at them. He kept his distance. He was not one of them. It was only when they finally got the lifeboat free that he turned and looked at them. Their lifeboat was now swinging out over the side of the ship, and they were struggling to lower it into the water. They were frightened, desperate men, and they stumbled and bumped into each other as they fought with the boat. Jim hated them.

"'I felt the ship move,' he told me. 'The front of the ship dipped and rose again. It was the first wave from the storm hitting the ship. I knew the end was near.

"'What would you have done? You're sure of yourself, aren't you? What would you do, right now, if you felt this hotel move a little under your chair? You would jump! I'm telling you—you would jump from where you're sitting and land in those bushes outside of the window.'

"I was annoyed that he asked me that question, and I didn't answer him. However, to be honest, I glanced toward the window and estimated the distance between me and the window. He was wrong. If I jumped, I would have landed several feet short of the bushes. That's the only thing I'm sure of.

"On the *Patna*, the end had come. Jim was sure of that. Still he did not move. Then, he saw the third engineer clutch at the air and fall down. He slid into a sitting position with his back against the side of the ship. The man had a weak heart. He had died of a heart attack.

"The storm was almost on them now, and finally the men struggling with the lifeboat managed to release it. The captain and the two engineers were in the boat when it fell into the water with a loud splash. They didn't know that the third engineer was dead, and they were calling him to save himself by jumping into the lifeboat.

"'By now it was so dark that you couldn't see the sky or the sea,' Jim went on. 'I heard the lifeboat bumping against the ship as it bobbed in the water. Then, the storm reached the *Patna*. The ship began a slow plunge, and the rain swept over the ship like a broken sea. My cap flew off my head, and my breath was driven back into my throat. It felt like the *Patna* was going down, down, head first under me.'

"As he told me all this, Jim raised his hand to his face and made a motion as though he were brushing aside a spider web. Then, he looked at his hand as if he expected to see something in it. He was silent for a moment, and then he said, 'I had jumped...'

"He looked away from me, then he turned and looked straight into my eyes. 'I didn't even know it—until I looked up and saw the *Patna* above me as I lay in the lifeboat. The ship loomed like a cliff over the lifeboat. There was no going back. It was as if I had jumped into a well—into a deep, dark hole.'

"He had indeed jumped into a deep, dark hole. It was so dark that the men in the lifeboat couldn't see each other. It was raining so hard because of the storm that they felt as though they might drown. It was like being swept through a cave by a flood, and the sea hissed like 20,000 kettles.

"He crouched in the front of the lifeboat and looked back at the *Patna*. One yellow light from the ship was still shining. The idea that the ship was still afloat terrified him, because that meant people were still drowning. He wanted the whole horrible thing to be over as quickly as possible.

"In the lifeboat, nobody made a sound. Then, someone said, 'It's gone!' They stood and looked back. They saw no lights. All was black. It was all over.

"'For a while everyone in the lifeboat stayed quiet,' Jim went on. 'Then, they started asking me why I had waited so long to jump. When they started calling me George, I realized they thought I was the third engineer, who died of a heart attack on the ship.

"'When they saw it was me, they were too surprised to say anything. What could I have said to *them?* Then, they started calling me horrible names. I could hear the hate in their voices. They hated the fact that I was in that lifeboat. They were angry that I hadn't helped them with it.

"'Their anger kept me from...Look! I was sitting on the edge of the lifeboat with my back to the sea. One little tilt backwards and I would have gone—after the others. That idea was in my head the whole time.

"'It was so cold. I'll never be so cold again in my life. The sky was black. Not a star or a light anywhere. They kept talking about me. They even accused me of killing the third engineer.

"'Then, they started to move as if they were going to attack me. I grabbed a piece of wood that was lying on the bottom of the boat, stood up, and dared them to try something. They backed away from me.

" 'I was ready for them. After the ship's lights disappeared, anything might have happened in that small boat—anything in the world. No one would ever know. We were like men walled up in a grave. There was no law but our own.'

"They were completely cut off from the rest of the world. Being alone in a small boat on the high seas can bring out both the best and the worst in people.

"In this case, nothing happened. However, when the sun rose in the morning, Jim was still standing, still holding the piece of wood in his hand, as he had all night. He had stood there, clutching it and ready for anything, for six hours.

"Can you imagine him silent, on his feet all night, and his face pelted by the rain? He was watching for any movement and straining his ears to catch their voices. Was it courage or fear?

" 'When the sun came up,' Jim continued, 'they were sitting there and staring at me like three dirty owls. Then, they said I could drop the piece of wood that I was holding. After all, they had done no harm to me.

"They wanted me to hear the story that the captain was making up for when we would be rescued. However, I didn't care about the story they would tell. No story would change any of this for me.

" 'Suddenly, I felt very tired. I dropped the piece of wood, turned my back on them, and sat down. I ignored them as they talked. I had had enough.

" 'I sat there for the rest of the day. They spread out the boat's sail and crawled under it to get out of the sun. I just sat in the sun for hours and thought. I was thinking about whether I wanted to live or die.' "

Chapter 5

Marlow continued his story. "'It's good of you to listen like this,' Jim said to me. 'You don't know what it is to have someone believe me. It's good for me to be able to tell my story to an older man.'

"I don't know how old he thought I was or how wise he thought I was. At that moment, however, I felt twice my age and only half as wise as I know I am.

"When we first go to sea, our hearts and minds are full of dreams. We're greedy for adventures. All of us who go to sea start out with the same dreams.

"That young man who sat before me believed that age and wisdom are a cure for the pain that the truth brings us. We may never see our dreams come true, and we may never have great adventures. For some people, nothing cures the pain that this truth causes.

"In the lifeboat, that poor young man had been deciding whether he wanted to live or die. He thought that he had saved his life—but now all his glory was gone with the ship that disappeared in the night. How could I not feel bad for him?

"Jim continued his story. 'Sitting in that lifeboat, I was so lost. You don't expect a thing like that to happen. It was like the story that the captain made up. It wasn't a lie, but it wasn't the truth. There wasn't the thickness of a sheet of paper between the right and wrong of this affair.'

"'How much more did you want?' I asked. However, I think I spoke so low that he didn't hear what I said. He just kept talking.

"'Suppose I stayed with the ship? At the time, I thought I would have been in the sea in 30 seconds. What do you think I would have done then? I would have grabbed hold of the first thing that I saw.

Wouldn't you? I would have intended to save myself. That's more than I meant to do when I. . .' he shivered as if he were about to swallow something terrible '. . .jumped.' He almost choked on his words.

" 'Now you understand why I didn't stay on the *Patna*. Even if I had stayed on the ship, I would have done my best to be saved. Men have been known to float for hours in the open sea without being hurt. I might have lasted longer than many others. There's nothing wrong with my heart.' He thumped his chest.

" 'So you escaped immediately,' I said.

" 'Jumped,' he corrected me. 'I couldn't see it then, but I had plenty of time to think about it in the lifeboat. I wasn't going to throw myself out of the lifeboat because of what I'd done. I wasn't going to run away. I might have at first. If it hadn't been for those three men, I might have. . .No, I would not! They wanted me to do that.

" 'They made up a story, but I knew the truth, and I would live it down alone. I wasn't going to let such an unfair thing get the best me. At that point, I was sick of life, but what good would it have done to kill myself? That wouldn't have solved anything. No, the proper thing to do was to face this, alone, and wait for another chance to find out. . .' He left that sentence unfinished.

" 'The *Avondale* picked us up just before sunset, and the others told their story. They said that there had been a slight shock to the ship, and that they stopped and looked at the damage. They also said that they did everything they could to lower the lifeboats without creating a panic. The others claimed that as the first boat was lowered, the ship went down in a storm and sank like lead.'

" 'You said nothing,' I whispered.

" 'What could I say?' he whispered back. 'I had jumped, hadn't I? That's what I had to live down.

Their story didn't matter.' He glanced right and left and looked into the gloom of the night around us. 'It was like cheating the dead.'

" 'There were no dead,' I said.

" 'Yes. Of course I was glad to hear that. I was relieved to learn that those shouts—did I tell you that I heard shouts? No? When I was in the lifeboat, I heard shouts for help. I thought it was my imagination. No one else in the lifeboat heard shouts, but *I* did.

" 'Yet, the lights on the *Patna* went out! If we had seen lights, I would have jumped out of the lifeboat and swum back. I would have had my chance.'

"The disappearance of the *Patna's* lights was discussed a great deal at the trial. The *Patna's* lights *had* disappeared. To the men in the lifeboat, that proved that the *Patna* had gone down. However, the real reason the lights on the ship disappeared was that the *Patna* had gotten turned around in the storm. Therefore, when the men in the lifeboat looked at the ship, the *Patna* herself was blocking the lights. It was as if the ship had turned its back on them just as they had turned their backs on it.

"The *Patna* did not go down. The next morning, a French gunboat found it drifting on a calm sea. The front of the *Patna* was tilted down, and the back of the ship was slightly out of the water. Someone on the *Patna* had the sense to hang the English flag upside down as a signal for help.

"All of the pilgrims were still on board. They were lined up at the rail—hundreds of them—silently staring as if a spell had been cast over them. After the captain of the French gunboat decided that the people on the *Patna* weren't sick, he sent a small boat over to see what was going on.

"Three years after all of this took place, I was in a café in Sydney,[13] and I happened to meet an old French naval officer. He had been on board that gunboat, and he remembered everything. In fact, many people remembered the *Patna* incident[14] and often talked about it. I've heard people still talking about it many years later and thousands of miles away from where it all happened. Aren't we talking about it tonight?

"I had never seen that Frenchman before, and I never saw him again. He and I talked about various things for a while, and before I knew it, we were talking about the *Patna*. He was one of the officers from the gunboat who boarded the *Patna*. They didn't know what had happened, and they were very confused when they found one dead man on the ship.

" 'It was impossible to understand,' he told me. He looked at the bulging bulkhead and decided that it could not be fixed. He advised his captain that the safest thing to do was to leave it alone. They attached two ropes to the *Patna* and towed her to the nearest English port. It was a delicate job, but luckily the sea was very calm and there was no wind.

" 'All the time we were towing the *Patna*,' the Frenchman told me, 'two men with axes were stationed near the ropes. They would cut us clear in case the ship suddenly went down. Those two men stayed at their posts for 30 hours. I stayed on the *Patna* for 30 hours, too.'

" 'You did?' I asked with surprise.

" 'It was the right thing to do,' he said quietly. 'I was an officer. We thought that an officer should remain on the *Patna* in case anything happened. So, for the next 30 hours, I was on the *Patna*.

" 'We towed the *Patna* to port, and in only 25 minutes, all of the people were taken off.'

---

13. Sydney the largest city in Australia
14. "Incident" refers to the crew of the *Patna* abandoning ship.

"He then told me that his ship had to leave for France at once, so there were many details about the incident that he never learned. 'What was this all about?' he asked. 'There were many strange things about it—like that dead man on the ship.'

"It seemed to me that he had a right to know. Hadn't he spent 30 hours on the *Patna*? Hadn't he taken over when the others abandoned the ship? Hadn't he done his duty? I told him what I knew of the incident, and he listened very quietly.

"When I finished, he said quietly, 'So that poor young man ran away with the others.'

"Suddenly, I was very glad to be talking about the *Patna* with this man. The old naval officer realized that this was the only part of the story that I really cared about. 'Ah, the young,' he said. 'After all, one does not die of it.'

" 'Die of what?' I asked.

" 'Of being afraid,' he explained. 'One is always afraid. We can say anything we want to, but there is always fear. Here.' He touched his chest and tapped the same place that Jim had touched on *his* chest when he told me there was nothing wrong with his heart. 'We all talk, but really, we are no more clever, and no more brave, than any other person.

" 'No, no, one does not die of it,' he said quietly. I was disappointed that he was not going to tell me the rest of his story, but it was not the sort of story that I could ask him to tell.

"We sat in silence for a while. Then, he said, 'People are afraid of things from the time they are born. It's hard to admit this, because you always worry about what people think of you. Sometimes people who are no better than you are do things that make them look brave. Therefore, you always want to look brave in front of other people. We can learn to accept the fact that courage does not come by itself. The honor—the honor, sir!—honor is important. I don't know how much life is worth when honor is gone.'

"'All right,' I said, 'but couldn't someone who has lost his honor just keep it a secret?'

"He looked as if he was going to respond very quickly but had changed his mind. Finally, he said, 'I don't know.' We nodded to each other in salute as we said good-bye, and he left the café.

"Anyway, Jim and I were in my hotel the day before the end of his trial. I told him about Captain Brierly's plan for him to leave town and run away, and I told him that I would give him some money. I also said that I'd be happy to write a letter to a man I knew in another country who could give him a job.

"He refused. 'Run away? I couldn't think of it,' he said while shaking his head. As I looked at him, I had the feeling that he was trying to prove to me that there was nothing wrong with his heart.

"By now it was very late, and he was getting ready to go. 'What will you do after the trial?' I asked.

"'Go to the dogs probably,' he muttered.

"'I'd like to see you after the trial,' I told him.

"'What will stop you? It's not going to make me invisible,' he answered bitterly. 'No such luck.'

"When the moment came to say good-bye, I realized his imagination had convinced him that I wouldn't want to shake his hand. It was too awful for words. Finally, with an embarrassed grin and a nervous laugh, he grabbed my hand in a crushing grip. As we shook hands, the candle on our table flickered out.

"He left and was swallowed up by the night. He was running, with nowhere to go to. He hadn't yet reached his 24th birthday."

Chapter 6

"The next morning I hurried to the court without visiting my ship, which I usually do. I was surprised that I felt so bad about what was going to happen. I was also surprised at how sunny it was. For Jim, this was the day that he was going to be sentenced. For everyone else, life went on as usual.

"The courtroom was gloomy and felt bigger than usual. Captain Brierly came in and sat down. He looked exhausted and seemed to be very nervous. He made quick little movements, as if he was stopping himself from standing up and urging us all to pray. I noticed he was pale, and looking at him made me think of a sick person sitting up in bed.

"He picked up a long sheet of paper and began to read out loud in a voice that showed no emotion. I felt as though he were about to issue a death sentence.

"During the trial, there had been several questions before the court. The first question was whether the *Patna* was fit for sea. The court had decided that it was not. The next question was whether the captain and crew had operated the ship properly before the accident. The court said yes to that.

"The court also declared that there was no evidence to show the exact cause of the accident. They decided the *Patna* had probably hit an abandoned ship that was floating in the water. Abandoned shipscan float below the surface like watery ghosts waiting to surprise other ships in the dark.

"Captain Brierly kept reading from his sheet of paper, and for a while I lost track of what he was saying. However, when I heard him say, 'Not doing their duty,' and then, 'abandoning the lives and property they were in charge of,' I looked at Jim.

"He sat very still, staring, listening to every word. The room grew very quiet. I was watching Jim so closely that I didn't hear the exact words Brierly spoke next. I did, however, hear that Jim's officer's certificate was taken away from him. Then, people started to leave the room.

"I waited for Jim outside and caught his arm to stop him. 'It's all over,' I told him.

"He jerked his arm from my grasp and walked away. He moved slowly and his legs wobbled as if he found it difficult to walk straight. Just before I lost sight of him, I thought I saw him stagger a little.

"'Man overboard,' said a deep voice behind me. Turning around, I saw a fellow I knew slightly. He was an Australian named Chester. He, too, had been watching Jim walk away.

"Chester had a large chest, a rough but clean-shaved face, and a thick mustache. He said that he had been everything a man may be at sea except a pirate.

"Right now, he was looking for a ship he could buy cheaply. He had discovered a tiny island covered with guano,[15] but going to the island was very dangerous. The waters around it were very rough, and there was no place to anchor a ship safely. He swore that the island was as good as a gold mine.

"Chester nodded toward Jim, who was walking down the street. 'He shouldn't be so upset by this,' Chester said. 'You can't take things to heart. If you do, you'll never do anything in this world.'

"'Look at me. I've got this great opportunity, and I can't get anyone to join me, even though it will make us all rich.' He went on and on, talking about many things at once. Every time I tried to get away from him, he caught hold of my coat and kept talking.

---

15. **guano** bird droppings. Guano is valuable because it is
    used as fertilizer.

"Finally, he said, 'I hear you know that young man.' He nodded down the street in the direction Jim had disappeared. 'Well, I've got something that's perfect for him. I'll give him a job on my guano island! I'm going to dump 40 workers on that island. I need someone to keep an eye on them to make sure that they work. I'll make him supreme boss over the workers. I want you to help me talk him into it. What do you say?'

"I didn't say anything. I imagined Jim perched on that tiny island, which was no more than a bare rock with no shade. I imagined him up to his knees in guano with the screams of sea birds in his ears, the blazing sun above his head, surrounded by the empty sky and the vast ocean, and nothing else as far as the eye could see.

"'I wouldn't advise my worst enemy. . .' I began.

"'It's too bad you won't help me,' Chester responded as he became angry. 'He'd be perfect for this. It's the perfect thing for him. I could guarantee that the island won't sink under him. I believe he has strong ideas about things like that! I was trying to do him a favor.'

"We said good-bye and went our separate ways, each of us angry with the other.

"I went looking for Jim and found him at the harbor leaning over the railing on the quay.[16] He didn't hear me walk up to him. When I touched him, he spun around as if he were on a spring. I asked him if he wanted to come back to my hotel.

"He followed me like an obedient child. He walked by my side in complete silence and he looked around, but he didn't see anything. I'm not sure that he even knew I was with him.

"When we got to my hotel room, I wanted to leave him alone so that he could think. To keep myself busy,

---

16. quay a wharf, usually built of concrete or stone, where ships are loaded or unloaded (pronounced key)

I sat down to write some letters. He had said that the trial would not make him invisible, and of course it didn't, but I behaved as though he were.

"Across the room there was a glass door that opened onto a balcony. He stood with his face to that door and did not make a sound. When it began to get dark, I lit a candle and moved carefully so that I would not disturb him. I could see that he was very upset. Once or twice I even thought that maybe Chester was right. Perhaps that tiny island in the middle of nowhere was the perfect place for Jim.

"I wrote letters for hours. Jim never moved from that window, but sometimes a shudder ran down his back and his shoulders lifted as he if was sighing. I could see that he was struggling, and he seemed to be fighting for breath. The room was quiet, but his swirling emotions made my own thoughts noisy and disturbed. I felt like a sailor in a storm when he's scared and he's glad he has the strength to get through it.

"Suddenly, I heard a low sound—the first sound I heard since we entered the room. Jim had pushed the glass door open. He pushed it so hard that the panes shook, and he stepped out onto the balcony. I held my breath and strained my ears without knowing what else I expected to hear.

"Did he intend to jump? He stood on the balcony and faced the dark night—a lonely figure on the shore of a sad and hopeless ocean.

"It made me so sad to watch him that for a second I wished that the court *had* given him a death sentence. If that had happened, all I would have to do for him now would be to pay for his funeral. Burying him would have been so much easier! Burying him would have made sense, because we usually put out of sight anything that reminds us of our weaknesses, fears, and failures.

"However, there was nothing I could do for him or say to him. In the future, I would see him loved, trusted, and admired. His name would become a legend of strength and power. He would win great honor and simple happiness in the jungle. Happiness can be found anywhere, and each of us decides what makes us happy.

"He did not gain his happiness quickly, however. First, he suffered, and I worried about him. The last time I saw him, he was happy. I will always remember him, though, as I saw him that night outside of my room when he was so upset by his failure.

"As he stood on the balcony, there was a heavy rumble of thunder, and suddenly the night was lit by the bright glare of lightning. He stepped in and closed the door behind him, and I found myself worried—almost frightened—about what he would say.

"When he did speak, he said, 'Well, I guess I got through that pretty well.' Hearing those words made me feel better. 'I wonder what's to come,' he continued.

"His face didn't show any emotion, but it looked dark and swollen—as if he had been holding his breath.

"He smiled and said, 'Thank you for letting me use your room.' Rain was falling outside as he spoke. 'It gave me shelter,' he said softly. 'I'm just a wanderer now.' He lowered his voice to a whisper. 'Some day I'll have the chance to get it all back again. I must!'

"I did not know what it was he wanted to get back or what it was he felt he no longer had.

" 'You know,' he went on, 'I feel as if nothing else can touch me. If this didn't finish me, then of course there'll be a time to get it all back. I've seen it through to the end, so I don't intend to let any man insult me about it.' He clenched his fist as he said this.

"Outside, the rain was falling hard. For some reason, I didn't want to let go of him. When he opened the door, I said, 'Wait, I want to talk to you.'

"I told him to come back and shut the door.

"I wanted to talk to him about his situation. He had no money, no job, no home, and no friends. He was still owed three weeks and five days' pay as mate of the *Patna*, but he would not accept that money. He made a gesture of horror when I mentioned it.

"I said I would help him. I don't pretend to understand what went on inside the parts of Jim that I could not see. His heart and his mind always seemed to be wrapped in a mist that never fully lifted. Yet, I could see his strong arms, shoulders, and back, and I wanted to help the part of him that I could see.

"I told him, 'I'm writing a letter to a man I know. I've never asked him for a favor before, but I'm asking him for a favor now. I'm asking him to give you a job.'

"He had been looking at the floor, but now he lifted his head. Outside, the rain had stopped, and the room was very quiet. In the soft light of my candle, his face seemed to be lit up, as if the night were over.

"'That is kind of you!' he sighed. His eyes were shining, and he moved about like an excited puppet on a string. He snatched my hand and shook it with great enthusiasm. 'You *have* helped me!'

"He went to the door, lowered his head in thought for a moment, and then came back. 'I always thought that if a man could begin with a clean slate...And now you...yes...a clean slate.'

"We said good-bye, and he marched out without looking back. I listened as the sound of his steps gradually died out. They were the steps of a confident man walking in clear daylight."

Chapter 7

"Six months later, I received a letter from the man whom I had asked to give Jim a job. His name was Denver. He owned a rice-packing plant, where Jim went to work. He said in his letter that he was happy with Jim and liked him so much that he asked him to live in his house. He said that whatever Jim had done, he was sure it could not have been very bad. After all, who hasn't done something wrong at one time or another?

"I was very pleased by this letter. It proved that I was right about Jim's character.

"When I returned from my next sea voyage, several letters were waiting for me. There was another letter from Denver, and I opened it first.

"'He is gone, and I have no idea why,' the letter read. 'He left a note on the table that said he was sorry.'

"I looked at the other letters, and there was one in Jim's handwriting! He wrote that he was now working as a water-clerk for the ship chandlers Egstrom & Blake, in a seaport 700 miles away from Denver's plant. The second engineer from the *Patna*, the man with the broken arm, had showed up at the plant and had taken a temporary job. So Jim had left.

"Jim had told his new employers that he knew me, and he was asking me to write a letter to them. I wrote the letter immediately, but I was very disappointed by what had happened.

"Several months later, my ship visited the port where Jim was now working. When I saw him, he told me what had happened. The engineer hadn't told anybody about the *Patna*. Still, he didn't treat Jim with the proper respect, and he acted as though they had a secret together. Then, one day, he asked Jim if he could have a permanent job at the plant. He hinted that he would tell Jim's secret. Jim hadn't told Denver about his past, and he was worried about what Denver would think of him.

"'I know that Denver liked me,' Jim said to me. 'He treated me like a son. I knew he'd be disappointed in me if I told him what had happened, so I preferred to go.'

"'You've thrown away a fortune,' I told him.

"'He was such a good man. How could I tell him?' said Jim. Then he walked away. He was off to meet a new ship in the harbor.

"I didn't see him again on that trip, but six months later I was back in the same seaport. When I went to Egstrom & Blake, they said Jim had left. They had no idea where he was now.

"'He left three weeks ago,' Egstrom told me. 'No use asking where. A man like that doesn't really go anywhere.'

"'Was anything said about the *Patna* incident?' I asked, fearing the worst.

"Egstrom looked at me as if I were a magician. 'Yes! How did you know? Some people came into the store and were talking about it. Jim was here, too, having lunch. One of the men had once done some repairs on the *Patna*, and he told us what an old ruin it was. Then, we all started to talk about her last voyage, and there was some laughing. One of the men, Captain O'Brien, called the crew of the *Patna* a bunch of skunks. He said they were a disgrace and that he would refuse to be in the same room as any of them. Just to be polite, I told him I agreed with him. Everyone laughed, and they all left.

"'Then, Jim stopped eating, came over to me, and said, "I'm leaving." I thought he meant that he was going back to work. When I realized he meant that he was quitting, I couldn't believe what I was hearing! It's very hard to get someone as good as him. Everyone said he was the best water-clerk in the harbor. I offered to pay him more. He just looked at me as if he wanted to swallow something that was stuck in his throat.

"'He said, "I can't stay here." I could see in his eyes that he was already as good as gone. I said to him, "Where are you getting to get a better job? This business isn't going to sink!"

"'He jumped when I said that. Then, he said, "If you knew my reasons for leaving, you wouldn't want me to stay."

"'I said that was the biggest lie he ever told in his life!' I told him, "If you keep doing this, you'll find that the Earth isn't big enough for you." He gave me the kind of look that would scare a child, and he walked out. How do you know him, anyway?'

"'Jim was the *Patna's* chief mate on that voyage,' I told Egstrom.

"He was very still for a moment, and then he exploded, 'Who cares about that? Why is he so upset about it? You see? I told him the Earth wouldn't be big enough for him!'

"This happened again and again. Some people might say that throwing away your job to wrestle with a ghost is the act of a hero. Yet, no matter how much of a hero he was in that way, he could not escape the shadow he was under. There would always be that secret. I could never decide if he was facing the ghost that haunted him, or running away from it.

"It was almost funny, because after a while everyone knew who he was and what he was running away from. He wandered through Asian seaports in a 3,000-mile circle, and everyone knew exactly who he was. He was becoming famous in an odd sort of way.

"For a while he worked in Bangkok.[17] The owner of the hotel where he lived was a man named Schomberg, who would take great pleasure in telling Jim's story to anyone who would listen. Even after hearing his story, everyone liked Jim.

"Jim was able to stay in Bangkok for six months. Then, a Danish naval officer got drunk and made an insulting remark about Jim. Most of the people who were in the room never heard the remark. The few people who did hear it could not remember it later. They were probably too frightened to remember it because of what Jim did next. He seized the officer and threw him off the hotel balcony into the river below.

"I was in Bangkok at the time, and Jim came to my ship. 'Everybody in the room seemed to know,' he told me. He was sorry for what he'd done to the Danish officer who, fortunately, had not been hurt. What really upset Jim was that his secret was known to everyone. It was as if he carried it on his shoulders in plain view. Now, he had to leave Bangkok.

"Even Schomberg, who almost never got angry, was disturbed by what Jim had done. 'Even though he's a very nice young man,' Schomberg said, 'I can't allow things like that to happen in my hotel. No, no! A man with a temper like that can't stay here.'

"I took Jim away from Bangkok on my ship, and it was sad to see how he shrank within himself. A sailor is always 'on deck.' Jim remained below. For whole days, we did not exchange one word.

"I found him another job, with a ship chandler named De Jongh. However, I was beginning to worry about him more and more. He seemed to be losing his confidence. One day, as I was coming ashore, I saw him standing on the quay, waiting for a boat. He said to me, 'This is killing me!'

---

17. Bangkok the capital and largest city of Thailand

"I knew very well that he wasn't referring to his job, because being a water-clerk was easy for him. 'Would you like to leave this part of the world and go to the United States?' I asked him.

" 'What difference would it make?' he asked.

"He was right. Going to another part of the world would not give him what he wanted. He was waiting for an *opportunity*. I had given him many, but they had been merely opportunities to earn a living. He wanted a different kind of opportunity. I decided to talk to Stein.

"Stein was a wealthy merchant. Yet, that was not why I went to see him. I went to Stein because he was a man who could be trusted, and I wanted his advice. He had a smile that made you feel that he was always ready to listen to you. He was a brave man who had often shown courage. His courage was simply part of who he was. He never even thought about it.

"Stein was also famous for his collections of insects. His collection of beetles contained tiny monsters that still looked dangerous, even though they were dead. His butterflies had made him famous all over the world. I felt that he was the perfect person with whom I could discuss Jim's problems, as well as my own."

Chapter 8

"That evening, Stein's gentle voice welcomed me to his huge study. The walls were covered with shelves that were lined with his dark boxes of beetles. His butterflies were in glass cases in three long rows on tables. When I entered the study, Stein was standing at his desk, staring at one of his butterflies.

" 'There is only one other specimen like this, and it's in London,' he said to me.

"Stein was born in Germany. As a young man, he had gotten into trouble and had to leave the country. He met a Dutchman who was famous for his knowledge of insects. The Dutchman hired Stein as an assistant and took him to Asia. They collected specimens of insects for more than four years. Then, the Dutchman went home.

"Stein had no home, so he stayed in Asia. He took a job with an old Scottish trader whom he had met on his travels. The trader treated Stein like a son. With his help, Stein did very well in business. Meanwhile, he collected every butterfly or beetle he could.

"Stein's life was going extremely well, and he was very happy. Then his luck changed, costing him his wife, his daughter, and everything he had. He lost it all, except for his butterflies and beetles.

"He started over, worked hard, and acquired a considerable fortune. Now, he owned a small fleet of boats and sold products from many different islands.

" 'Look at this,' he said to me, still staring at the butterfly. 'It's marvelous! So delicate and so strong. Nature is in perfect balance. Nature is a great artist.'

" 'What about people?' I asked.

" 'People are amazing but not as perfect.'

" 'I captured this rare specimen one very fine morning,' he told me. 'You can't know what it is for a collector to capture such a rare specimen.' His eyes took on a faraway look as he began his story.

" 'One night many years ago, when I was a young man, I got a message that a friend needed to see me at his house. His house was ten miles away, and there was a war going on at the time, so going to see my friend was very dangerous. Still, I set out on my horse early the next morning. My wife did not want me to go. I told her that I would be careful.

"'I rode for four or five miles, and suddenly somebody fired 20 shots at me. It was a trap. My enemy had made my friend send for me, and then he set this trap to kill me. However, they had fired too soon. They should have waited until I was closer.

"'I fell forward and let my head rest on my horse's neck, to make it look as if I had been shot. My horse kept walking forward, and I could see where they were hiding. They thought I was dead, so they came out of their hiding place to capture my horse.

"'I let them come close, and then—bang, bang, bang—I shot three of them. The last man got away.

"'I sat on my horse, looking at the three men lying on the ground. As I looked for some sign of life, I saw a faint shadow pass. It was the shadow of this butterfly.

"'I got off my horse, still holding my revolver. I walked very slowly, looking up, down, right, and left. Finally, I saw the butterfly sitting on a small heap of dirt ten feet away. My heart began to beat quickly.

"'I let go of my horse, kept my revolver in one hand, and with my other hand, I snatched my hat off my head. I crept up on the butterfly, and flop! I dropped my hat over it, and I got it!

"'I was so excited that I shook like a leaf. When I opened these beautiful wings and saw what a rare, special, perfect specimen I had, my head spun. My legs got so weak with happiness that I had to sit down. I had always wanted this specimen. I even dreamed about it. Now I had it in my hands!

"'My friend, on that day I had everything I wanted. I had defeated my enemy, I was young, and I was strong. I had a wife who loved me, I had a child, I had friends, and I had the thing I had dreamed about!'

"Stein struck a match to light his pipe, and the match exploded into flame. He stared at the flame and became thoughtful. 'Friend, wife, child,' he said softly. Then he blew, and the flame was gone. 'Now, what did you want to talk about?'

" 'I came here to talk about a specimen.'

" 'A butterfly?'

" 'Nothing that perfect. A man.' He listened carefully as I told him about Jim. When I finished, he laid down his pipe and said, 'I understand very well. He is a romantic.'[18]

"He had described Jim perfectly, and I suddenly realized that we were like two doctors discussing a patient. 'What's the cure for it?' I asked.

"Stein lifted up a long finger. 'There is only one cure. People have to find it within themselves.

" 'This magnificent butterfly finds a little heap of dirt and sits still on it. A man will never sit still on his heap of mud. He wants to be so many different things. Every time he shuts his eyes, he imagines he's someone finer than he can ever be.

" 'We can't always live in our imagination. Sooner or later, we have to return to the real world. When we realize that we can't live up to our dreams, it hurts. It's not good to learn that we can't make our dreams come true. We say, "I'm a fine fellow! How can this be?" Ha-ha! This terrible thing is very funny.'

"We spoke for a long time. Then, Stein said, 'Sleep here tonight. In the morning, we'll do something about him.'

"As Stein showed me to my room, he said, 'He is romantic. That is very bad. ...That is very good, too.'

"When we reached my room, I said to Stein, 'You dreamed of a butterfly. When you had the chance to

---

18. romantic a person who has big ideas and perfect dreams, but who is not realistic make your dream come true, you didn't let the opportunity escape. He has....'

"Stein lifted his hand to stop me. 'Do you know how many opportunities I *did* let escape? How many dreams came my way that I lost?' He shook his head. 'Perhaps even *I* don't know how many. Everybody has opportunities that they have missed. That causes us all great trouble. Sleep well. Tomorrow we'll do something for him.' "

Chapter 9

Marlow stopped telling his story for a minute. Then, he went on, "I'll bet none of you has ever heard of Patusan.[19] Well, it doesn't matter. Nobody has. Some people who work for the government know it, and a few traders know it by name. I don't think any of them would ever want to go there. Jim did go there. Stein arranged it, and he could not have sent Jim farther away if he had sent him to a distant star.

"Stein mentioned Patusan to me the morning after we talked about Jim in his study. I told him what Brierly said about Jim: 'Let him creep 20 feet under the ground and stay there.'

"When I said that, Stein looked at me with great interest—as if he were looking at a rare insect. 'That could be done,' he said.

" 'You mean, bury him?' I asked. Stein nodded.

"Stein owned a trading post in Patusan that was managed by a man named Cornelius. Stein was very unhappy with Cornelius and wanted to replace him. That was what he had in mind for Jim.

---

19. Patusan (pronounced PAH-too-son) a fictional country based on Conrad's travels. Conrad located Patusan in northwestern Sumatra. Sumatra is one of the islands that make up modern Indonesia.

"What Stein and I were trying to do was get Jim out of the way. Get him some place where he'd be safe, especially from himself. I had another reason, too, for talking to Stein about helping Jim.

"I was going home to England for a while. Jim had come to me from England. I could go home, but Jim could not. I wanted to go home with a clear conscience, knowing that I had done everything I could for him.

"Our lives mean something only when we stick together and help each other. Jim was one of us, so I had to help him. Our lives had touched. I didn't want his life to be completely ruined, and I was afraid it would be ruined if I didn't help him. Stein's solution was to send him to Patusan.

"Patusan was a small settlement in a remote part of a distant country. It was reached by going 30 miles up a river into the jungle. I wouldn't know a thing about Patusan, if Stein hadn't told me about the place. He knows all about it because he owns the only trading post there.

"When Jim went to Patusan, three people were battling for power there. One was Rajah Allang, who was an uncle of the country's young ruler. The Rajah controlled the river that led to Patusan, and he stole anything he could from the people who lived there. These people were poor Malays who had no defense against Rajah Allang.

"I met Rajah Allang when I went to Patusan to see Jim. The Rajah had evil eyes, stringy hair, and a wild look about him. He received Jim and me in a big old house with a rotten floor. There were cracks in the floor, and you could see garbage under the house. There were a lot of people walking in and out of the house, and it was extremely noisy.

"Jim looked very confident and made quite an impression on everyone. His clean white clothes and blond hair glowed in the sunlight, and he looked as if he might have come from another world. If those people hadn't seen him arrive in a canoe, they might have thought he'd come down from the sky.

"He did arrive in a canoe, of course. On his lap was a revolver that I had given him. For some reason, he had decided to carry it without bullets. That's how Jim went up the river to Patusan.

"Neither Stein nor I had any idea what would happen to Jim when we sent him there. I simply wanted to get him out of sight. Stein had his own reason. He had always been very friendly to anyone from England. This was his way of repaying the Scottish trader who had treated him like a son. Now Stein was passing on to a young man the help that he had received in his own young days.

"When I told Jim about Patusan, I was very honest about the place. He was being offered a refuge, but that refuge was full of danger. I even made the danger sound worse than it might have been.

"As things turned out, Patusan was even more dangerous than I said it was. Jim's first day there was almost his last. It *would* have been his last if he had loaded the revolver that I gave him.

"As I told Jim about Patusan, he became more and more excited. He said this was the chance that he had been dreaming of. He thanked me. He became a little embarrassed when he mentioned that I had always trusted him. He said that he would never give me a reason to regret my faith in him.

"I warned him that he was going into the wilderness and would be entirely on his own. Whatever might happen, there would be no one to help him. He would be completely ignored, because the rest of the world didn't care what happened in Patusan. It would be as if he had never existed.

" 'Never existed! That's it!' he murmured, his eyes sparkling.

"I told him that if he still wanted to do this, he should go to Stein's house for his final instructions. He raced out of my hotel room the second I finished speaking.

"When Jim came back the next morning, the first thing that he did was tell me what a wonderful man Stein was. Jim now had a letter that he was to give to Cornelius, the man at Stein's trading post whom Jim was going to replace.

"Stein also gave Jim an old silver ring. This was his introduction to a man named Doramin, who was one of the three powerful men in Patusan. Stein and Doramin were old friends who had fought together many years ago. Stein had saved Doramin's life, and Doramin had given Stein this ring the last time they saw each other.

"The ring was a promise of friendship, which both men had vowed would last forever. The ring would tell Doramin that Jim was also Stein's friend. 'It's like something you read about in books!' Jim said.

"He didn't want to lose the ring, so he hung it around his neck. He said the ring meant that he had a friend. 'It's good to have a friend,' he said, looking straight at me. Then, he became quiet and thoughtful.

"Soon he was excited again, pacing around the room as he did on the night he tried to explain what had happened on the *Patna*. 'This is what I've been waiting for!' he almost shouted. 'I've been dreaming of it! I'm ready for anything!'

"I couldn't help wonder what he was excited about. All that was going to happen was that he was going to manage a trading post in a far-off place. I found myself a little annoyed with him. I told him he was approaching this with the wrong attitude.

"He thought about that for a moment. He told me that even I—who had been so kind to him—even

I remembered what he had done. Of course, everyone else would remember it, too. Why should it surprise me that he wanted to get out of the world and stay out? How could *I* talk about having the wrong attitude?
" 'It's not I or the world who remembers,' I shouted. 'It's you!'
"Now, he was angry. 'I'll forget everything and everybody!' he said. Then his voice fell, and he added, 'Except you.'
"We were both quiet for a while. Then, he began talking again. He was calmer now and said that he would never come back from Patusan.
" 'Don't be silly,' I told him. 'Sooner or later, you'll want to come back.'
" 'Come back to what?' he asked. I had no answer.
"One of Stein's ships was setting sail that day, and Jim would be leaving on it. I had some things to do on my ship, and later, Jim came to say good-bye. A revolver and two boxes of bullets were lying on my table, and I gave them to him. He thanked me and rushed out, calling good-bye over his shoulder.
"After he left, I saw that the boxes of bullets were still on the table. I grabbed the bullets and went after Jim in one of my ship's boats. Jim was so excited that the men rowing his boat must have thought he was crazy, and their lives were in danger. They rowed so fast that by the time I was half-way to Jim's ship, I could see him climbing over the rail and going on board. When I reached the ship, Jim was below in his cabin.
"The captain of the ship told me he was taking Jim to the mouth of the river that led to Patusan, but he would not go up that river. If Mr. Stein ordered him to go up the river, he would quit. He had been to Patusan the year before. He went up the river then, and his ship had been shot at. Patusan was a dangerous place, he said, with people who could never be trusted.

"Jim came up on deck, and we said good-bye again. He finally responded to my concerns for his safety. 'I promise to take care of myself,' he said. 'I won't take any risks. I feel as if nothing could touch me, but I wouldn't spoil such a magnificent chance!'

"It was a magnificent chance for him. As he had said, even I remembered what he had done on the *Patna*. It was true—the best thing for him was to go.

"As I returned to my vessel, I saw Jim standing at the rail of his ship. He raised his cap high above his head, and I heard him shout, 'You shall hear of me!'"

Chapter 10

"The coast of Patusan faces a misty ocean. The jungle is cut by trails of red earth that look like rusty waterfalls when you see them from the ocean. There are swamps where the rivers flow into the sea, and jagged peaks that tower above the forests.

"I went to Patusan two years later and was taken up the river to the settlement in one of Stein's boats. My boat was guided up the river by an old man who was the head of a fishing village. The old man told me that Patusan was a lot safer than it used to be. The place had been greatly changed by a man who came from the outside world two years ago. He called him Tuan Jim, and he said that his village was under Jim's special protection. That showed what a good man Tuan Jim was, since the people of his village had betrayed him when he arrived.

"Jim had said I would hear of him, and now I was. There was already a story being told that when he came here, the tide had changed direction two hours early, to help him go up the river.

"When Jim arrived in their fishing village and demanded to be taken up the river, they didn't know what to do, the old man told me. What would the Rajah do to them if they helped the stranger? They feared the Rajah, but they also feared the anger of this stranger. So, they decided to take him up the river.

"Jim sat in the boat with the empty revolver on his lap. He was very tired, and it was very hot. He told me later that he passed the time trying to figure out if the muddy things he kept seeing in the water were logs or alligators. He soon gave that up, because they were always alligators. Meanwhile, the men from the fishing village who were paddling his boat were taking him to the Rajah instead of to Patusan.

"'Maybe I fell asleep, or maybe I was so tired that I didn't know what was going on,' Jim told me. Before he knew it, the men paddling the canoe were steering it toward a small stockade. Then, they leaped out of the canoe and ran off.

"Jim heard excited shouts, and the gate of the stockade swung open. People poured out, running toward him. At the same time, a boat full of armed men came alongside his canoe, cutting off escape.

"'I was startled,' he told me, 'and if that revolver had been loaded, I would have shot two or three of those men. Then, they would have killed me. I just stood there, and that surprised them. I was told that the Rajah wanted to see me, and here I am!'

"He laughed and said, 'Do you know what the best part is? It's knowing that if I had been killed, this place would have been the loser.'

"He told me this story as we stood in front of his house in Patusan on a moonlit night. Two hills rose high above the settlement, and the full moon glowed red as it floated in the sky between these hills. 'It's very pretty, isn't it?' Jim said, full of pride.

It sounded as if he felt that he himself had created that beautiful arrangement of moon, sky, and hills.

"We could see red gleams of light inside the houses in the settlement. Jim told me that he often watched these tiny gleams go out one by one. He loved to see the people go to sleep under his eyes, confident that they were safe. 'Look at these houses,' he said. 'There's not one where I am not trusted and respected!' I could see how much it meant to him to be here.

"The next day, Jim showed me around the Rajah's stockade. 'I was prisoner here for three days,' he murmured. 'I gave up that revolver of yours as soon as they demanded it. I was glad to get rid it. I looked like a fool walking around with an empty gun in my hand.'

"When I met the Rajah, I saw that the evil old man was afraid of Jim. He didn't even try to hide it. It turned out that he was no hero, even though he liked to tell stories about the brave adventures of his youth. I also saw that even though the Rajah hated Jim, he trusted him.

"Jim began to lecture the Rajah about the behavior of some of his men. The Rajah's men had robbed some people while on their way to Doramin's house to do some trading. Jim wanted the Rajah to understand that no man should be prevented from getting food for his family.

"The Rajah sat with his head low, looking at Jim through the long, stringy gray hair that fell over his eyes. When Jim finished speaking, no one made a sound. The Rajah sighed, looked up, and said to the people standing near us, 'You hear, my people! No more of these little games.'

"Then, one of the Rajah's men brought us two cups of coffee on a brass tray. 'You don't have to drink,' Jim muttered to me. I didn't know what he meant at first, but then it struck me—there was a chance that the coffee was poisoned! Jim took a big sip of coffee and sat very calmly. Shortly after, we left the Rajah. "As we climbed into a canoe to return to Patusan, Jim said that he was very sorry about the coffee. 'If I'm to do any good here, drinking the Rajah's coffee—even though it might be poisoned—is a risk I must take. I do it at least once a month. The Rajah is afraid of me—most likely because I'm not afraid of his coffee.'

"He showed me a fence made of stakes, and pointed to a part of the fence where the pointed tops of several stakes were broken. 'That's where I jumped over the fence on my third day in Patusan. Good leap, eh?'

"A moment later, we passed the mouth of a muddy creek. 'That was my second leap,' he told me.

"Jim's arrival in Patusan was a complete surprise to the people who lived there. That's what saved him from being immediately stabbed with krises[20] and flung into the river. The Rajah's men had captured him, but they did not know what to do with him.

"Should they kill him at once, or try to please him? Why had someone from the outside world come to a miserable place like Patusan? Was a foreign power coming to conquer the country? They even asked him if he wanted to leave, although they never said that he could. The Rajah nearly went crazy trying to decide what to do with Jim. He and his advisors argued about it night and day.

"After three days, Jim realized that he was in danger and decided to do something. While walking across the stockade, he saw the fence with the broken stakes. Without thinking about what he was doing, he began his escape. Taking a running start, he leaped

---

20. **kris** a Malayan dagger with a wavy double-edged blade

over the fence and landed on the other side. Behind him, there was a great yell. Ahead of him, about 1200 feet away, he could see the houses of Patusan.

"He started running toward the houses, but he came to a creek that blocked his way. He ran to the edge of the creek and jumped. He landed, feet-first, in the soft, sticky mud of the bank of the creek. He desperately grabbed at the creek bank, but the mud gave way. He was soon covered from his chest to his chin with horrible slime.

"As he clawed wildly at the mud, it fell on his face, and into his eyes and mouth. It felt as if he was burying himself alive. Suddenly, the Rajah's stockade seemed like a safe place, and he wished he were back there again. He made a tremendous effort and finally freed himself. He ran, covered with slime, toward the houses of Patusan.

"As he ran through the settlement, women fled before him and old men stared at him, terrified. He kept running until he blundered into the arms of several startled men. He had just enough breath to gasp out, 'Doramin! Doramin!'

"He was taken into a big courtyard and brought before a huge man sitting in a chair. He fumbled through his muddy clothes to find Stein's ring. Suddenly, he was on his back. He wondered who had knocked him down, but they had simply let go of him. He was no longer able to stand up on his own.

"He heard shots outside the settlement, but he was safe. Doramin's people were blocking the gate. Someone was pouring water down his throat. 'They put me to bed,' he told me, 'and I just lay there like a log for I don't know how long.'

"Doramin was the second of the three powerful men in Patusan. He was an immense man with proud eyes, and his entire appearance was a display of dignity.

He dressed in richly-colored silks and wore a red and gold cloth around his huge head.

"He spoke in a deep murmur that sounded as if it came from a distance, and he never raised his voice. Once he sat down, he hardly ever moved. When he walked, two young men held his elbows. They would ease him down and stand behind his chair.

"When he wanted to rise, he would turn his head slowly to the right and left, and they would help him up. However, there was nothing weak about him. His body was powerful and he had a spirit of iron.

"Doramin's son was a highly respected young man. His name was Dain Waris, and he was about 24 years old. Dain Waris and Jim became very close friends. Jim told me, 'He is the best friend I ever had, except for you.'

"Doramin was the chief of about 60 Malay families who had come to Patusan from the nearby island of Celebes.[21] He commanded about 200 fighting men. His followers were the Bugis people, and they opposed the Rajah. All of the disputes in Patusan were about trade. The Rajah insisted that he was the only one in Patusan that people could trade with. However, when the Rajah traded with people, it was the same as robbing them.

"The third powerful man in Patusan was Sherif[22] Ali, the religious leader of the people who lived deep in the jungle. He had built a stockade on top of one of the hills that rose above Patusan.

"Many of Patusan's young men wanted to ally themselves with Sherif Ali and drive the Rajah out of the country. For many years, Doramin had stopped this from happening, but he was growing old. The constant struggle for power in Patusan was beginning to be too much for him.

---

21. **Celebes** one of the islands that make up modern Indonesia (pronounced SELL-eh-bees)
22. **Sherif** a Muslim title of respect (pronounced sheh-REEF)

"This was how things were in Patusan when Jim was brought before Doramin and showed him Stein's silver ring. 'Soon after that,' Jim told me, 'I suddenly saw what I had to do. I had the power to make peace. The Bugis were afraid. They were caught between the Rajah and Sherif Ali. They had to do something immediately, or they'd all be killed off.'

"Jim had to convince the people of Patusan that he was right. He had to come up with a plan that would work. Then, he had to persuade them to act.

"Dain Waris was the first to believe in him. A small but powerfully built man, Dain Waris had great courage. He didn't talk very much, but he was intelligent and appeared to always be thinking. He not only trusted Jim, but he seemed to understand him, too.

"Doramin had several old cannons. Jim's plan was to haul the cannons up one of the hills behind the settlement. Sherif Ali's stockade was on the other hill. Once the cannons were in place, they could fire on the stockade and blow it to bits.

"Getting the cannons to the top of the hill was extremely difficult. Jim and the men from the settlement struggled all night to drag and push the guns up the hill.

"Doramin himself was carried up the hill in his chair, so he could watch his people work. 'They put him down on a level place on the slope,' Jim told me, 'and he sat with a pair of enormous pistols on his knees. They were black pistols, trimmed with silver, which were a present from Stein, in exchange for that ring. He sat there, not moving at all, while everyone rushed about, shouting and pulling.

"'He wouldn't have had a chance if Sherif Ali's men attacked us, but he had come up there to die if anything went wrong. It thrilled me to see him there, solid as a rock. Sherif Ali must have thought we were crazy, so he never came to see what we were doing. Nobody believed it could be done. Even the men pulling and dragging those cannons didn't believe it could be done!'

"Jim had taken me to the top of the hill to tell me this story. He stood there in the bright sunshine, with a smile on his lips and a sparkle in his boyish eyes, tall and proud, like a statue looking down on the forest. By this time, Jim was already a legend in Patusan. Some people even said that he had carried the cannons up the hill on his back, two at a time.

"After working all night, they finally got the cannons to the top of the hill. They decided they would fire on Sherif Ali's camp when the sun came up. While it was still dark, Jim and Dain Waris led a group of Bugis to the edge of Sherif Ali's camp. They hid in a ravine.

"It was extremely important to Jim that his plan work. He had given his word to the people, and they trusted him. 'As far as I know,' he told me, 'I have never given them a reason to regret their faith in me.'

"The people's trust was very important to Jim. He even wondered if they trusted him too much. They called upon him to settle every little dispute, and they did whatever he told them to do. Since the defeat of Sherif Ali, his word decided everything in Patusan.

"When the sun came up and the cannons were fired, the men hiding in the ravine attacked Sherif Al's camp. Jim and Dain Waris were the first to storm the camp. People were now saying that Jim knocked down the gate with the touch of one finger.

"The truth was that Sherif Ali's stockade was not very well built. Sherif Ali thought he didn't have to worry about an attack, because he had built his stockade at the top of the hill. In addition, the cannon fire had already blasted the camp, so there wasn't much left of it by the time the Bugis attacked.

"Jim threw his shoulder against the gate and tumbled into the camp head over heels. As he lay on the ground, one of Sherif Ali's men attacked him with a spear. If Dain Waris hadn't been there, Jim would have been pinned like one of Stein's beetles.

"The third man into the camp was Jim's servant, Tamb' Itam. This man was a Malay who had found his way to Patusan by chance. He had been immediately taken prisoner by the Rajah. At his first opportunity, he escaped and took refuge in the settlement. When Jim arrived, Tamb' Itam offered himself to Jim as a servant.

"Tamb' Itam was extremely devoted to Jim and followed him everywhere like a shadow. He often had one hand on his kris. The look in his eyes was a warning to everyone that they had better not even think of trying to hurt his master.

"Jim had made him the head servant in his home, and now the people of Patusan treated Tamb' Itam with great respect. When Sherif Ali's stockade was attacked, Tamb' Itam impressed everyone with how well and how bravely he fought.

"The battle for Sherif Ali's camp lasted only five minutes. The fighting was fierce, but it ended quickly when someone set fire to the camp and everyone had to run from the smoke.

"The attack was a complete success. As he stood on the hill after the battle, Jim could hear the people celebrating in the village below him.

" 'You must have enjoyed it,' I said to him.

" 'It was...immense! Immense!' he cried, flinging his arms open. 'Immense!' he repeated in a whisper, as if the third time was just for himself.

"After the attack, Sherif Ali fled the country. The Rajah's reaction to Jim's victory was total fear. When he heard what had happened, he threw himself face down on the floor and lay there for a whole night

and day. He was worried that Jim would attack him next. Jim was now thought of as someone who could not be defeated.

"If not for Jim, the Bugis would have attacked the Rajah. They wanted revenge for everything the Rajah had done to them in the past. The only thing that saved the Rajah from the Bugis was Jim's opinion that they did not have to attack the Rajah to make him leave them alone.

"With Sherif Ali gone, the Rajah terrified, and the people of Patusan willing to do whatever he told them, Jim was, in effect, ruler of the land.

"Doramin's dream was that his son would rule Patusan in the future. He expected Jim to leave Patusan some day. He told me that he was hoping that when he died and Jim left, Dain Waris would rule Patusan. All it would take to make Dain Waris ruler of Patusan was one word from Jim.

"'Outsiders come here,' Doramin said to me, 'but they always go back to their own land. Tuan Jim will leave some day.'

"'No, no, he will not leave,' I said.

"Doramin wanted to know why.

"I was unprepared for this. This happened on the last day I was in Patusan. Strangely enough, that very night I was asked the same question again. Why would Jim want to stay in Patusan? This brings me to the story of his love.

"The man who had managed Stein's trading post in Patusan was named Cornelius. He was the man Jim came to Patusan to replace. Cornelius had been married to a woman who died many years before. That woman's first husband was a man from the outside world who went back to his own land, leaving the woman with a young daughter.

"When Cornelius married this woman, he gained not only a wife, but a step-daughter as well. By the time Jim came to Patusan, Cornelius's wife was dead and her daughter was a grown woman. Jim called her Jewel, and she became his wife.

"I heard her name for the first time only ten minutes after I arrived at Jim's house in Patusan. He nearly shook my arm off when he said hello, then darted up the steps and, like a little boy, called out, 'Jewel! Jewel! A friend has come!'

"Minutes later, a woman with delicate features and intelligent eyes peered out of the house, like a bird in a nest. When Jim called her Jewel, something I had heard on the way to Patusan suddenly made sense.

"There was a story making its way around the region about a mysterious man from the outside world. He had an enormous green gem that was priceless. The man, who was very strong and cunning, had taken the gem from the ruler of a distant country.

"He arrived in Patusan running for his life. He frightened the people there with his great power, which could not be defeated. A gem like this, I was told, is best preserved by being concealed on the body of a woman. Not just any woman—she had to be young, wise, and completely loyal.

"There was a woman like that in Patusan, and the man from the outside world treated her with great care and respect. They walked together every day, arms around each other, and she carried the man's great jewel hidden beneath her clothes.

"The story was pure imagination and was all wrong, of course. Except for one thing—Jim did not hide his jewel. In fact, he was extremely proud of her.

"Dark, flowing hair framed her pretty face, and she moved with wonderful grace. While Jim and I talked, she was always watching Jim. I should say she was watching out for him, as if looking for some danger.

"She never went to sleep until Jim and I said good-night. I often saw them through the window of my room, talking quietly outside the house, his arm about her waist, her head on his shoulder.

"I could also hear something else as I lay in bed. I heard faint breathing outside of the house, and I knew that Tamb' Itam was still on the prowl.

"Tamb' Itam was always with Jim, marching right behind him. He carried many weapons, including a kris, a lance, and Jim's gun.

"On the evenings when Jim and I sat up late, talking on the porch, Tamb' Itam would silently walk back and forth or stand off to the side in the shadows. Then, he would vanish without a sound. However, when we got up, he would spring up close to us, as if rising from the ground, ready for any orders Jim might wish to give.

"Tamb' Itam hardly ever said a word, but he was always watching. One reason was Cornelius, whom he did not like at all.

"Cornelius was always creeping about. He was often seen circling slowly among the sheds or passing in front of a house and casting sneaky glances all around him. His walk resembled the creeping of a beetle.

"Jim didn't seem to give much thought to Cornelius. He acted as though he didn't have enough respect for Cornelius to even consider him dangerous. Jim left the settlement soon after he arrived in Patusan. It wasn't safe for him to leave the village yet, but he felt it was his duty to look after Stein's business. With no care for his safety, he crossed the river and moved into Cornelius's house.

"'Even his house was disgusting,' Jim told me. 'Half the roof had fallen in, and the entire house was horribly dirty. Cornelius claimed that Mr. Stein owed him money for the last three years' trading, but his account books were all torn, and some were missing. Trade-goods were missing, too. There was nothing in the storehouse but rats.'

"Jim's first six weeks in Patusan were difficult. He told me, 'After I escaped, the Rajah was frightened and returned all of my things. However, as soon as I left the Bugis and went to live with Cornelius, I heard that the Rajah was going to have me killed. The worst of it was, I felt I wasn't doing any good for Stein or for myself. It was terrible.'"

Chapter 11

"Jim told me he didn't know what made him stay in Cornelius's house. I know that he stayed partly because of his feelings for Jewel. She had a terrible life with Cornelius. He demanded that she call him Father and treat him with respect. 'Do you think I am going to bring up somebody else's child and not be treated with respect?' he would yell at her. He shouted terrible things about Jewel's mother and threw mud in Jewel's hair.

"Jim would have enjoyed giving Cornelius a beating. He told Jewel he would do that if she wanted him to.

"Her answer surprised him. She said she would have killed Cornelius herself, except that she knew he felt completely miserable about himself and his life.

"Leaving Cornelius's house would have meant abandoning Jewel, and Jim couldn't do that. While he lived there, he sensed that there was danger all around him. Twice, Doramin sent a servant to tell Jim that he could not protect him unless he crossed the river and lived in the village with the Bugis. People kept coming to Jim's door in the middle of the night with warnings about plots to kill him. He was going to be poisoned, stabbed, or shot at from a boat on the river.

"One night, Cornelius told Jim that for $100, or even $80, he would smuggle Jim down the river to safety. Cornelius made a great show of being worried for Jim. When Jim refused, Cornelius squealed, 'Your blood is on your own head!'[23] and rushed away.

"Jim did not believe Cornelius, but he admitted to me that he did not sleep that night. He lay on his mat, staring at the ceiling. On that very night, he thought of his plan for defeating Sherif Ali. Suddenly, he could see it all, and he became very excited.

"He jumped up and went out on the porch. Jewel was there, standing very still against the wall as if keeping watch on a ship. When he told her about his plan, she said she thought it was a very good idea. However, she was on the alert all the time.

"Suddenly, she pressed his arm and walked away. Cornelius appeared, and seeing Jim, he ducked sideways, as if he had been shot at. Afterward, he stood very still in the dark.

"Finally, he came forward, moving like a suspicious cat. 'There were some fishermen here to sell fish,' he said in a shaky voice.'

"It was 2:00 in the morning. Who would sell fish at that hour?

"For some reason, Cornelius was very nervous. He held the rail of the porch with both hands, as if he could not stand up. Jim had a lot to think about, so he went into the house and lay down on his mat.

"Soon, he heard soft footsteps outside, and a voice whispered nervously through the wall, 'Are you asleep?'

---

23. You will be responsible for whatever happens to you.

"'No,' he answered. 'What is it?' There was a quick movement outside, as if the whisperer had been startled. "Annoyed, Jim stamped back to the porch, and there was Cornelius. He let out a low shriek and ran away. Then, he called to Jim from the darkness. 'Have you given any thought to what we talked about?' He sounded as if he was shivering or shaking with a fever.

"'No!' shouted Jim, 'and I don't intend to. I am going to live here, in Patusan.'

"'You will d-die h-h-here,' answered Cornelius, still shaking.

"At that moment, Cornelius seemed to represent all the difficulties Jim had found in his way. He shouted at Cornelius, calling him every name he could think of.

"Jim told me about this as he, Jewel, and I sat on his porch. He said he was embarrassed that he let Cornelius make him so angry. What finally made him stop shouting was Cornelius's silence. Cornelius was doubled over the porch rail, Jim said, 'As if he had died while I was making all that noise.'

"Jim went back to bed and slept better than he had in weeks. 'I didn't sleep,' Jewel told me. 'I watched.'

"Jim spent the next day with Doramin, persuading him to try his plan to attack Sherif Ali. There was a big meeting of the important Bugis. Jim left the meeting very happy about how convincing he was when he spoke to them.

"When he crossed the river and returned to Cornelius's house, Jim was feeling so good that he tried to be civil to Cornelius. As they sat in the house and talked, Jim grew annoyed by Cornelius's little squeaks of false laughter. Jim hated to see Cornelius smile and twitch and look back at him with a blank stare.

"When Jim rose from his chair to say good-night, Cornelius jumped up, knocking his own chair over. He ducked out of sight, as if he had dropped something. When he stood and looked at Jim again, his mouth hung open. He had a stupid, frightened look in his eyes. He acted so strangely that Jim asked if he was sick.

" 'Yes, yes, yes. A bad pain in my stomach.' he answered.

"That night, Jim dreamed he heard a voice telling him to wake up. When he opened his eyes, he saw a red light and thick black smoke curling around a figure dressed all in white. It was Jewel. She was holding a lantern and repeating, 'Get up! Get up! Get up!'

"He leaped to his feet, and she pressed his revolver into his hand. This time, it was loaded.

" 'There are four men,' she said, talking fast and low.

"He followed her out of the room, and she led him toward the trading post's main storeroom. It was a long hut built of mud and clay, with a wide door at one end and a small window with three wooden bars in one of its walls.

"Jewel whispered, 'They were going to attack you while you slept.'

"At first, Jim thought it was another false alarm about a plot to kill him. He became angry with Jewel for bothering him. He had followed her because he thought she wanted his help, but now he was ready to turn on his heel and go back to bed.

" 'They're in the storeroom,' Jewel whispered, 'waiting for the signal.'

" 'Who's supposed to give the signal?' he asked.

" 'You've been sleeping so badly,' she continued without answering, 'they didn't know if you were asleep. I've been watching you sleep, too.'

" 'You?'

" 'Do you think I watched you only tonight?'

"His heart was thumping, not with fear but with excitement. He heard the grass rustle, and he stepped out of the light. Something scampered out of sight. He called out, 'Cornelius!' but there was only silence. "Jewel said, 'They're frightened. They know you're awake now. They know you're big, strong, and fearless.' " 'If I am all that...' he started to say, but she interrupted him. " 'Yes, tonight! What about tomorrow night, or the next night, or all the nights to come? Can I be always watching?' He thought he heard her crying. 'Go to Doramin,' she whispered.

"In that moment, he realized how lonely he would be without her. He thought, 'If I go away from her, it will be the end of everything.'

"He made up his mind to go into the storehouse. As he approached it, he muttered to himself, 'I am fearless, am I?'

"He let Jewel follow him without thinking about it, as if they were one person. When he reached the door, she laid her hand on his arm. 'Wait until you hear my voice,' she said.

"She ran around to the side of the storehouse. He stood in the darkness, facing the door. Not a sound came from the other side. Then, he heard Jewel calling to him: 'Now! Push!'

"He pushed the door hard. Inside the storehouse, he saw the smoke and glare of the lantern. Jewel had thrust the lantern through the bars in the window. The only other thing he saw was a large pile of old mats in the corner that rose almost to the ceiling.

"He was bitterly disappointed. It was another false alarm after all.

" 'Fire! Defend yourself!' Jewel yelled at him. Standing outside, with her arm thrust through the small window, she couldn't see what was going on inside.

"'There's nobody here!' yelled Jim, about to laugh at how silly it all was.

"Just as he was turning to walk out of the storeroom, he saw a pair of eyes staring at him from the pile of mats in the corner. The mats moved, and with a scowl and a low grunt, a man rushed at him. His right arm was raised above his head, clutching a kris in his fist.

"Jim waited until the man was only inches away from him. Then he fired.

"The explosion of the shot was enormously loud. The man fell at Jim's feet. The storehouse was full of smoke from the lantern, which Jewel still held, completely steady.

"Jim stepped over the body on the floor and aimed his revolver at another man he saw in the corner. The man dropped his spear and squatted silently against the wall in surrender.

"'How many more are there?' Jim asked.

"'Two more, Tuan,' said the man very softly. Then, two men crawled out from under the mats, holding out their empty hands."

Chapter 12

"Jim took the men out of the storehouse and marched them to the edge of the river. Jewel walked by Jim's side, holding the lantern. Her white gown trailed behind her, and her long black hair fell to her waist. She seemed to be gliding over the ground without touching it.

"When they reached the river, Jim said, 'Take my greetings to Sherif Ali—until I come myself. Now, jump!' They leaped into the river and dove deep, afraid that Jim would fire at them as they swam away.

"Jim turned to Jewel, who had not said a word all this time. He loved her so much that he felt his heart might burst. They stared at each for a long time, until he finally found words for what he was feeling. He never told me what he said to her.

"On my last day in Patusan, Jim said to me, 'I've lived here only two years, and I can't imagine living anywhere else. The very thought of the outside world scares me.

"'I haven't forgotten why I came here,' he went on. 'It's strange. These people would do anything for me. If you asked them who is brave, who is true, who is just—who it is they would trust with their lives— they would say, Tuan Jim. Yet, they can never know the real truth. . . .

"'It's over, and I like that. I can think about it and not be upset. I've got my confidence back. I haven't done so badly. Yet. . .you wouldn't want me as a mate on *your* ship, would you?'

"'Stop this!' I shouted at him.

"'See?' he cried, as if he had just proved something. 'Only, try to tell that to anyone here. They'd think you were a fool, a liar, or worse. I've done a thing or two for them, and this is what they've done for me. Well, I will always stay here.'

"It was night, and Jim, with Tamb' Itam close behind, of course, went off to make his evening rounds of the village. I was going into the house, when Jewel suddenly appeared. She had been waiting for the chance to talk to me alone.

"It's hard to tell you, as we sit here, what she wanted from me. The best way to describe it would be to say that she wanted me to promise her something.

"She had grown up in Patusan and knew nothing of the outside world or its people. Her mother had come from the outside world, and so had Cornelius.

Now, Jim had come to her from there. What would become of her if Jim went back to the outside world?

"I, too, belonged to this outside world, and I believe she thought that with one word I could take Jim from her. She thought, perhaps that was what he and I were discussing. I think she was so afraid that I would take Jim from her, that she might have been willing to kill me if it would keep her from losing Jim.

"She moved her arms as she talked, and the wide sleeves of her gown rose in the night like unfolding wings. Her youth and beauty had the simple, delicate charm of a wildflower. However, there was an enormous strength about her, even as she feared what she didn't know—as we all do.

"I wasn't sure what to say to her, but I told her at once that I did not intend to take Jim away.

"'They always leave us,' she murmured.

"I told her that Jim would never leave her. She answered, as if speaking to herself, 'Yes, he swore that to me, too.'

"She then told me that *she* had asked Jim to leave Patusan. That night on the riverbank, after he had killed the man in the storehouse and ordered the other three to jump into the river, she asked him to leave. She felt he was in great danger if he stayed. She would rather lose him and see him live, than have him stay and see him killed.

"He told her that he would not leave; he would not abandon her. When she insisted that he leave, he told her that he could not—that it was impossible. She felt him tremble when he said this.

"When Jewel asked Jim to leave Patusan, she was trying to save him from being killed. She was also trying to save herself from something. She said to me, 'I don't want to die weeping like my mother.'

"I was very touched by this. Her mother had been in love with a man from the outside world, and he had left her. Now, Jewel was in love with a man from the outside world. If he left her, she, too, would die weeping.

"'He swore he would never leave me when we stood at the river!' she whispered softly.

"'Don't you believe him?'

"'Other men have sworn, too. My father did.'

"'Jim is not like that.'

"'Why is he different? Is he better? More true?'

"'I believe he is more true than any other man' I told her. 'Nobody here would doubt his word—except you. What has he told you?'

"'He told me that there is something he can never forget. He says he was afraid. Yet, how can I believe this? All of you outsiders remember something! You all go back to it. What is it? What is this thing? Is it alive? Is it dead? Does it have a face? A voice? Will he see it? Will he hear it—maybe in his sleep when he cannot see me—and then go? If he does that, I shall never forgive him.'

"She waited for me to explain it all to her. I would have given anything to be able to help her. She was so afraid, like a small bird beating its wings against the cruel wires of a cage. All I could say was, 'He will never leave here. Don't be afraid of that.' How could I make her understand? How does one kill fear?

"I told her there was nothing in that outside world, living or dead—no face, no voice, no power—that could tear Jim from her side. 'When he told you that he would never go, he told you the truth.'

"'Why did you come to us from out there?' she asked me. 'He speaks of you too often. You make me afraid. Do you want to take him away?'

"'No, I don't. No one wants him to leave here.'

"'No one?' She found that hard to believe.

"'No one. You think he is strong, wise, brave, and great. Why don't you believe him to be true, as well? I'm leaving here tomorrow, and I will probably never come back. He loves you. The outside world is too big to miss him. It has forgotten him. It doesn't want him.'

"'Why?' she murmured.

"'Because he is not good enough,' I said quietly.

"I felt her hand clutch my arm with a powerful grip. 'That's exactly what *he* said! You're lying!' She flung my arm away, and I thought I heard her crying.

"'Nobody is good enough...' I started to say. Then, I heard Jim returning, and I walked away toward the house.

"'Hello, girl!' he called out to her.

"'Hello, boy!' she answered, her voice sounding strong and happy.

"It was their usual greeting to each other. This was the last time I heard them say it, and for some reason, it chilled my heart.

"When Jim saw that Jewel was alone, he called out to me, but I didn't answer. After my conversation with Jewel, I couldn't act as if nothing had happened.

"Instead of going into the house, I walked around to the side. The night was so quiet that it seemed as if all movement in the world had come to an end.

"Suddenly Cornelius scampered out of a clump of tall grass, like a huge insect. He ran toward me. I'd always had the feeling that he wanted to talk to me in private. He was always lurking about with an eager, hungry look on his sour face—but I never wanted to have anything to do with that disgusting creature.

"This time, I didn't try to avoid him. He just didn't matter anymore. Jim had told me that he was satisfied with his life...or nearly satisfied. That's more than most of us can say.

"I could almost envy him for his disaster, since this is what it led him to! He was nearly satisfied. Now, it did not matter who suspected him, who trusted him, who loved him, or who hated him—especially since it was Cornelius who hated him.

"Jim didn't think Cornelius mattered. The day I left Patusan, Jim told me, 'The worst Cornelius can do is kill me. I don't think he could do that if I handed him a loaded rifle and turned my back on him. Even if he did kill me, so what? I didn't come here to save my life.'

"That was the last time Jim and I talked. We were sitting in his boat as he took me down the river on the day I left. Tamb' Itam sat right behind him. I had mentioned Cornelius, and Jim was a little angry that I had.

"I was telling Jim what Cornelius had said to me the night before, after I talked with Jewel. As soon as he had reached me, Cornelius began to whine and shake. He told me that he was the most unhappy man on Earth, and that he been crushed like a worm.

"He tried to explain to me why he had helped Sherif Ali try to kill Jim. He was just doing what he had to do so he could live! 'I would have saved Jim,' he sputtered. 'I would have saved him for $80!'

"'He saved himself, and he's forgiven you.'

"Cornelius laughed when I said that. 'Don't be fooled by him! Who is he? What does that big thief want here? He throws dust in everybody's eyes. He throws dust in *your* eyes. Yet, he can't throw dust in *my* eyes. He's a fool. He's no more than a little child!'

"I'd had enough of Cornelius, and I walked away. He caught up with me and finally squealed out what he wanted. He wanted me to talk to Jim for him. He wanted money in exchange for Jewel. He had raised her, and if Jim gave him some money, he would take care of her again when Jim went home.

"As he said this, his eyes squeezed together. I could see greed in every part of his crumpled little face.

" 'Jim will never go home,' I told him.

" 'He'll never go? Oh, this is no good!' he shouted. 'He came here to trample on me until I die? Well, I will not be trampled on!' he whispered, leaning his awful face close to mine. 'Ha-ha-ha! We shall see! We shall see!' Then, he rushed away. He shouted something over his shoulder, but all I heard clearly was, 'No more than a little child!'

"I told Jim all this the next morning as he took me down the river. I was going back to the world he had given up. He was going to remain in this wilderness.

"As his boat glided down the river, paddled by 20 men, I was very aware of the hot, still air, the dampness of the thick mud, and the smell of the rich earth.

"Then we suddenly reached the sea, and everything changed, as if a huge door had been thrown open. The sky above us was bigger, the sea stretched out before us with no limit. Sea air filled our lungs, and I could feel my heart beat faster.

"I took a deep breath of the fresh clean air and said, 'This is glorious!'

"Jim sat with his head sunk on his chest and said, 'Yes,' without raising his eyes.

"We landed on a small beach. Nearby was the fishing village that was under Tuan Jim's protection. Now, two men paddled over to us in a canoe. They were coming to see Jim because the Rajah's men had given them trouble about some turtle eggs that the people from the village collected.

"As soon as Jim knew what they wanted, he told them to wait. They nodded and went off to the side to wait silently for him.

" 'The trouble is,' he told me, 'that for generations these poor fishermen have been fair game for the

Rajah's men. The Rajah can't get it into his head that I've changed all that.'

" 'You've had your *opportunity.*'

" 'Yes,' he said. 'I've got back my confidence in myself. Yet sometimes I wish that I could....No! I will hold on to what I have. I can't expect anything more.' He flung his arm out toward the sea. 'Not out there, anyhow.'

"As we walked along the beach, he said, 'Imagine what would happen here if I went away! No! Tomorrow I will go and take my chances drinking the Rajah's coffee and make a great fuss about those turtle eggs. These people believe in me. I must stick to their belief in me to feel safe, and to...' he seemed to search for a word and lowered his voice...'to keep in touch with those I may never see again. With—with— you, for instance.'

"He didn't look at me. For the first time, he let his eyes wander across the wide, open sea. The sun was beginning to set, and the water had changed from blue to gloomy purple.

" 'Then, there's Jewel,' he said very quietly. 'She trusts me, too.'

"Suddenly his voice changed. 'When shall you and I meet next, I wonder?'

" 'Never,' I answered, avoiding his eyes. 'Unless you come out.' He didn't seem to be surprised.

" 'Good-bye, then,' he said, after a pause. 'Perhaps it's just as well.'

"We shook hands. I walked to the small boat that had come to take me out to the ship.

" 'Will you be going to England soon?' Jim asked, as I climbed into the boat.

" 'In a year or so,' I told him. The men in my boat pushed off from the shore and began to row toward the waiting ship.

"Jim raised his voice. 'Tell them...' he began. Then, he stopped. 'No, nothing,' he said. With a slight wave, he motioned the boat away.

"I did not look at the shore again until I was on board the ship. By that time, the sun had set. The shore was wrapped in darkness that seemed to build a wall around it. Out toward the horizon, the sky was one great blaze of gold and bright red.

"I saw Jim on the beach, watching my ship sail away. He was dressed in white from head to foot. The light was fading in the sky above him, and the strip of sand on which he stood was sinking from sight. He appeared to be no bigger than a child. Then, I lost him."

Chapter 13

That was the end of Marlow's story. The men who had been listening to him rose from their chairs and walked away in silence. The story had no ending, and they seemed to feel that there was nothing to say.

All of the men who heard the story that night had their own thoughts and feelings about it. There was only one man among them who would hear how Jim's story finally ended. This man would not hear the ending until two years later.

He was at home one day when he received a package in the mail. When he opened the package, he found three items inside.

The first thing he found was a stack of papers in Marlow's handwriting. The second was a sheet of gray paper with a few words written on it in a handwriting he had never seen. The third thing he found was a letter from Marlow. Inside Marlow's letter was another letter, written on old, slightly torn paper that had turned yellow with time. The man read Marlow's letter first.

"Of all the men sitting on the porch that night, listening to Jim's story," Marlow's letter began, "you showed the most interest. So, I'm letting you know how the story ended.

"Perhaps what finally happened to Jim was the last test, the one that I always thought he was waiting for. You can decide for yourself. The world will hear no more about Jim, and those who do hear his story will decide for themselves how they feel about him.

"Jim made one effort to tell his own story, as you'll see from the sheet of gray paper in this package. The handwriting is his, and the address on the paper is headed: 'The Fort, Patusan.'

"The fort was Jim's house. After I left Patusan, he turned his house into a fort. He dug a deep ditch and built an earth wall around it. On top of the earth wall were platforms with guns mounted on them. He wanted to give the people a refuge and a place to fight from if Patusan was ever attacked.

"He also let the people who had been Sherif Ali's prisoners live in Patusan under his protection. Jim called them 'my people,' and they were loyal to him.

"I don't know to whom he was writing when he took up his pen—perhaps Stein, perhaps myself, or perhaps no one. As you can see, he wrote, 'An awful thing has happened.'

"I've also sent you a very old letter that was found among Jim's belongings. It's from his father. According to the date on the letter, Jim must have received it a few days before he joined the crew of the *Patna*. It's the last letter he ever had from home.

"From the letter, it's clear that Jim's father loved him a great deal. I noticed one sentence in which his father tells him, 'Never do anything that you believe is wrong.' The letter also has other advice about how to live, as well as lots of news about Jim's family.

"I found it strange to think of Jim as once being part of an ordinary family. Like most people, their lives were full of minor concerns. Also, like most people, they did not have the kind of adventures that Jim had. They would never have to make a single decision that would affect the rest of their lives.

"The stack of papers in this package will tell you how Jim's story ended. You'll find it to be romantic beyond the wildest dreams he had as a boy. It's an astounding adventure.

"Yet, astounding as it is, when you think about who Jim was, and how he lived, something like this had to happen. I've written it here as if I saw it all myself. The truth is, I heard it in bits and pieces, from several different people in many different places.

"It all begins with a man named Brown. I happened to meet him just a few hours before he died. By the time I met Brown, I knew what had become of Jim. Brown told me the part of the story I didn't know yet.

"Brown was obviously dying. When we spoke, he could hardly breathe, he coughed constantly, and he kept choking. Still, the very thought of Jim made his body shake with vicious laughter.

"He seemed to take great pleasure in the thought that he had gotten even with Jim. He bragged about what he had done, and I had to listen to his gleeful boasting to learn what happened. The story he told me proved what an evil person Brown was. It also showed how cunning and truly horrible Cornelius turned out to be.

" 'As soon as I saw Jim, I knew what a fool he was,' Brown told me, gasping for breath. 'He was a fake! Why couldn't he just say to me, "This country and these people belong to me! You can't have them!" That's what a real man would have said! He thought he was so much better than me! He had me trapped, but he wasn't man enough to finish me off. He let me go, as if I wasn't worth the trouble to kill or even to fight.

"'From what you've just told me, it appears that *I* finished *him* off! I'm dying now, but I'll die happy because of this news.'

"I had found Brown in Bangkok, in a dirty little hut. A ragged blanket was wrapped around him. He died later that night, but by then I had heard his story. Before I tell you that story, I want to go back eight months, so that I can tell a different part of this tale.

"Eight months before I met Brown in Bangkok, I found myself in the city where Stein lived. Of course, I went to see him. On Stein's porch, I saw a Bugis trader I knew from Patusan. When I went inside Stein's house, Tamb' Itam was standing outside Stein's study. I thought that perhaps Jim had come to see Stein.

"'Is Tuan Jim here?' I asked Tamb' Itam.

"'No,' he mumbled, hanging his head. 'He would not fight. He would not fight.'

"I went into Stein's study and found him alone, standing between the rows of butterfly cases. 'Ah, is it you, my friend?' he said sadly. 'Come and see Jewel. She is here. She and Tamb' Itam came two days ago.'

"Stein led me at once to Jewel. As we approached the room she was in, he said to me, 'Young hearts don't forgive easily. She can't understand me. I am only a strange old man. However, she knows you. Perhaps you can talk to her. Tell her to forgive him.'

"When I entered the room, Jewel said to me very quietly, 'He has left me. You people always leave us. You are all hard and scheming. Without truth and without feelings for others. What makes you so wicked? Is it that you are all insane? He shall have no tears from me,' she whispered. 'Not one tear. He went away from me, as if I were worse than death. He fled from me, as if he were driven by some terrible thing he had heard or seen in his sleep.'

"I took her hand, but there was no life in it. When I let it go, it fell to her side as if it were not part of a living thing. Her complete lack of response was more awful to me than tears or anger would have been. I felt that nothing I could say would ease the cruel pain in her heart.

"When I finally left the room, she made no sign that she even saw me go. Her eyes seemed to be searching for the shape of a man torn out of her arms by the power of a dream.

"I sat alone in Stein's garden for a while, thinking about what Jewel had said. Later, I saw Stein and Jewel walking in the garden.

" 'You must forgive him,' I said to her. Then, I added, 'We all want to be forgiven.'

" 'What have I done?' she asked.

" 'You never trusted him.'

" 'He was like the others,' she said slowly. 'He was false.'

" 'No! No! No! My poor child!' Stein said. 'Not false! True! True! You don't understand. Some day you will understand.'

"Tamb' Itam, the Bugis trader, and Jewel had escaped from Patusan in the trader's boat. The shock of what happened had changed them.

"Jewel behaved as if she had turned to stone. Tamb' Itam, who never talked in Patusan, now talked all the time. He was also humble and puzzled, as if something that he thought had magical power failed when it was needed most. Both Tamb' Itam and the Bugis trader seemed to be filled with a deep, silent wonder, as if they had been touched by a mystery that they would never understand."

Marlow's letter ended here. The man who received the package immediately began to read the stack of papers that told the rest of the story.

"It all begins, as I said in my letter, with the man called Brown," Marlow's story read. "You've traveled all over the Pacific Ocean, so you must have heard of him. They tell all sorts of stories about this awful criminal everywhere. Even the least of his terrible deeds could get a man hanged.

"He was a terror on the seas, a savage pirate who hated everyone. Brown was especially cruel to anyone unfortunate enough to become one of his victims. He robbed and killed people just for the fun of it.

"He was finally captured and faced a long term in prison. Brown would not have cared if he faced a death sentence. He was not afraid of death, but he was terrified of being put in prison. The very thought of being locked away made him break out in a cold sweat. So, he made up his mind to escape.

"While he and his men were being held temporarily, he managed to get away. He stole a ship, and with 15 of his men, he fled for his freedom across the open sea.

"They had guns and a large supply of ammunition, but they had very little food or water. With a stolen ship, Brown did not dare to enter a port. His men stole what they could from the small boats they met on the ocean, but it wasn't enough. They became desperate.

"Perhaps Brown had heard of Patusan, or maybe he just happened to see its name on a map. He did know it was a village that could not defend itself, and it was so far away from the rest of the world that he could do whatever he wanted there. It was the perfect place for him to take his stolen ship and the hungry, cruel men who followed him.

"Only a few days after he escaped, Brown dropped anchor near the fishing village at the mouth of the river that led to Patusan.

"He and 13 of his men packed into the ship's small boat and started up the river. Brown left 2 men behind to watch the ship. They had enough food for ten days.

"When their small boat reached Patusan, Brown was surprised at how big the settlement was. He saw that a stockade on the bank of the river was quiet, and the first houses that came into view seemed empty. Brown thought he had the element of surprise on his side. His plan was to take over the village before anyone could even think of resisting him.

"However, it was Brown who was surprised. The chief of the fishing village had sent a message to Patusan, warning that Brown was coming. The Bugis were waiting for him. Two small cannons were fired at Brown's boat from up the river. People began shouting, and then the men of the village, who were hidden on both sides of the river, fired volleys [24] of shots at Brown's boat.

"While Brown's men rushed to protect themselves and row the boat to safety, Brown sat, amazed and enraged that these people dared to defend their village. Two of his men were wounded. Then, his retreat was cut off when six boats, full of the Rajah's men, came up behind him from down the river.

"Brown noticed a narrow creek. It was the same creek that Jim jumped over when he escaped from the Rajah. Now it was full of water. Brown steered his boat in, and his men climbed out quickly.

"There was a hill about 900 yards from the Rajah's stockade, and they ran to it. Once they were on top of

---

24. volley a burst of a number of weapons discharged at the same time the hill, they had a good position from which to defend themselves.

"They quickly cut down the few trees that were growing there, piling them up for protection. When the sun set, Brown ordered his men to set fire to the grass around them. After the grass was burned away, they could easily see anyone coming up the hill. Brown expected the Rajah's men to attack or at least take his boat, which was down the hill on the bank of the creek. However, the Rajah's boats remained where they were in the river.

"As they lay on the hill in the dark, Brown and his men could see many small fires that had been lit by the Bugis along the river. Boats were crossing the river from one side to the other.

"Once again, Brown found himself surprised at how immense this place was. From where he lay, the settlement seemed to go on forever. It appeared to be swarming with thousands of angry men. Now and then, the men on the hill heard a yell or a single shot ring out, fired by someone far away. Yet, all around them, everything was still, dark, and silent. They seemed to be forgotten, as if they were already dead.

"Jim was away from the settlement when Brown arrived. Dain Waris wanted to attack the invaders and kill them immediately. However, he couldn't get the village leaders to agree with him. He didn't have Jim's reputation for being a man whom no one could defeat. Jim could not be killed, they believed, but Dain Waris could be killed. Nobody in the village wanted that to happen.

"With Brown's men trapped on the hill, the leaders of the town met in Jim's house to talk. If Jim could not be with them, perhaps they might find wisdom and courage in the place where he lived. They assembled around a long table to decide what to do.

"While Jim was gone, Jewel was in charge of his house. Jim was the only one in Patusan who had gunpowder. Jim had given Jewel the key to the storehouse where the gunpowder was kept.

"At the meeting, Jewel sided with Dain Waris. She, too, wanted to attack the invaders immediately. Standing next to Jim's empty chair when she spoke, she was beginning to persuade the village leaders to attack.

"If Doramin had said he agreed with Jewel, the Bugis would have attacked Brown. However, Doramin did not say that he agreed with Jewel. He knew that Dain Waris would lead the attack, and he did not want to risk losing his son.

"Then, someone argued that if the invaders stayed on their hill, they would starve. If they tried to escape in their boat, they would be shot and killed by men hiding along the river. So, the Bugis did not have to risk a battle.

"The village leaders thought this made a lot of sense. They also were surprised that the Rajah's men had not attacked the invaders when they had the chance earlier that day.

"At this meeting, the Rajah was represented by a man named Kassim. He listened with a friendly smile to everything that was said. He spoke very little, and nobody could tell what he was thinking.

"During the meeting, reports kept coming in about the invaders. Most of the reports were wild rumors. Some people thought there was a large ship at the mouth of the river, with big guns and many more men. Everyone was very afraid. At one point, one of the Bugis shot at something moving on the river and

nearly killed a man from the village who was bringing his family to the fort. This caused more confusion.

"Later in the meeting, Kassim said that the Rajah's boats would be called back from the river, because the men were needed to defend the Rajah's stockade. Finally, it was decided that armed men should be sent to the houses nearest the creek, so they could watch Brown's boat. The boat was not to be attacked or taken, because it was hoped that the men on the hill would try to escape. Then, the Bugis could shoot them down.

"Doramin ordered Dain Waris to take an armed party of Bugis ten miles down the river. They were to make camp and block the river with canoes. This would cut off the escape of the invaders and prevent more invaders from coming up the river. That's what Doramin said. However, I think he just wanted to keep his son out of harm's way.

"Of course, men were sent to find Jim. They started out when the sun rose. By then, Kassim was having his own meetings with Brown.

"When he left the meeting of the village leaders, Kassim found Cornelius shuffling about among the people gathered outside. Kassim took Cornelius with him. He had his own plan for dealing with Brown, and he wanted Cornelius to talk to Brown for him.

"In the morning, Brown was sitting on top of the hill, thinking about how desperate his situation was. Then, he heard Cornelius's shaking, squealing voice, asking if he could come up the hill on a very important mission. This made Brown very happy. If these people were speaking to him, he was no longer a hunted wild beast.

"Brown told Cornelius to come up. When Cornelius came into view, Brown's men stared at him. All their hopes hung on this cowardly, shabby stranger.

"After half an hour's talk with Cornelius, Brown had learned a great deal about Patusan. He saw that there were immense opportunities for him in this place. Before he would talk more with Cornelius, he demanded some food for his men.

"Cornelius went to the Rajah's stockade. A little later, some of the Rajah's men brought up food. Cornelius followed. This time, Kassim was with him, and the three men talked for a long time.

"Kassim hated Doramin and his Bugis, but he hated the changes that Jim had brought to Patusan even more. He thought that if Brown's men and the Rajah's men joined forces, they could defeat the Bugis before Jim returned. Then, Jim would have no more power in Patusan. After that, the Rajah's men could easily get rid of these invaders.

"Brown had his own plan. He had come here thinking that he would steal what he could and be on his way. Now, he began to think about stealing the whole country.

"This other outsider, Tuan Jim, whom everyone kept talking about, had apparently done something like that already. However, he had done it by himself. Perhaps Brown could work with this outsider, and together they could squeeze the country dry.

"His talk with Kassim made him realize that these people thought he had a big ship with plenty of men down the river. Kassim kept asking him to have his ship brought up the river and placed in the Rajah's service. Brown told Kassim he was willing to do this.

"In the afternoon, Brown got more food from the Rajah. He also got a promise of some money and some mats so his men could make shelters for themselves. Protected from the burning sun, Brown's men lay down and slept. Brown, however, sat in the open sun, looking at the town and the river. There was much to steal here, he decided.

"Cornelius, who now stayed in Brown's camp, told Brown more about Patusan and more about Jim. 'He is a fool,' Cornelius said. 'All you have to do is kill him, and then you are king here. Kill him the first chance you get, and you can do what you like.'

"Earlier in the day, Dain Waris's fleet of canoes went down the river to set up their camp. Brown did not know about this, and when Kassim came up the hill again, he did not tell him. He wanted Brown's ship to come up the river, and he was afraid that if Brown knew about Dain Waris, he might not do it.

"Kassim urged Brown to bring his ship up and offered to send a messenger to the ship to deliver Brown's order. He told Brown that he would have the messenger travel on land instead of on the river to keep the trip secret.

"Brown told Kassim that he was writing the order. Instead, the message he sent to the men on his ship read, 'Keep this man on the ship.' The young man whom Kassim picked to deliver the message was never seen again.

"Thinking that Brown's ship was coming, Kassim sent a message to Dain Waris, warning him to look out for the invader's ship and to attack it.

"Kassim wanted to keep the Bugis forces divided, to weaken them by having them fight and lose men. Meanwhile, he also sent word to the Bugis leaders that he was trying very hard to persuade the invaders to retreat back down the river.

"Brown kept talking with Kassim, but he was really waiting for Jim. His plan was to join forces with Jim. He would make it easier for Jim to run things. They would work together like brothers until Brown could force a quarrel and kill Jim.

"While he waited for Jim, Brown pretended to be on Kassim's side, so he could get food for his men. He was even willing to do some fighting for the Rajah. He would enjoy killing a few Bugis, to get even with these people who had dared to welcome him with shots. What he really wanted to do was burn the village to the ground, just because it had resisted him.

"From the top of the hill, the village appeared to be deserted. Yet, in every house, armed men waited on the alert. Suddenly, a lone man came walking along between two buildings. Brown saw the man and realized that he thought he was far enough away from the invaders to be safe.

"Brown called one of his men over to him. This man was the best shot Brown had, and when he understood what Brown wanted him to do, a big smile spread across his face. He dropped to one knee, took careful aim with his rifle, and fired.

"The man walking in the village fell to the ground, dead. 'That showed them what we could do,' Brown told me. 'It put the fear of sudden death into them, and that was what I wanted. The odds against us were 200 to 1, but that showed them. Nobody there had ever seen a shot from such a long distance before. It terrified every one of them!'

"Darkness came, hiding the body of the dead man. The sky was lit with countless stars, and the settlement was lit up by fires blazing along the street.

"It was very quiet, except for the noise that came from a large fire in front of Jim's fort. To Brown, this noise sounded like the stamping of hundreds of feet, the hum of many voices, and the roar of a distant waterfall.

"Brown later confessed to me that right then, he felt that perhaps he had gotten himself into a situation that he would not get out of. He admitted to me that if there had been enough water in the creek for his boat to float, he would have tried to get away. He would have taken his chances with a long chase down the river and perhaps starving at sea.

"He also thought of attacking on the town, but he knew that he and his men would be shot down like dogs.

"Then, one of Brown's men remembered that there was some tobacco in their boat. He crept down to the boat to get it. A moment later, there was the sound of a gunshot. 'I'm hit!' shouted the man.

"All the rifles on the hill went off as Brown's men fired back.

"When it was quiet again, a voice called up the hill from the river. It was one of the Bugis, declaring that between the Bugis and the men on the hill, there would be no faith, no sympathy, no talk, and no peace.

"The long shot that had killed the man earlier that day had indeed terrified the Bugis. It also stirred them to anger. They were outraged by how vicious that shooting had been, and now there could never be peace between them and these invaders.

"Later that night, Brown heard a small cannon go off somewhere in the town. Then, a big drum began to throb, and other drums responded. 'He has come,' said Cornelius.

" 'Why are they making all that noise?' Brown asked.

" 'For joy,' snorted Cornelius. 'Jim is a very great man. Yet, he knows no more than a child does, so they make a great noise to please him. He will come to talk to you, and you will see what a fool he is. He is not afraid of anything. He will come and order you to leave his people alone. Then, Mr. Brown, you must tell that man with the rifle to shoot him.'

"Cornelius was almost dancing with joy as he said this. 'Kill him, and you will frighten everybody so much that you can do anything you like here. Ha-ha-ha! Kill him!' "

Chapter 14

"The next morning, Brown saw a crowd of silent people moving through Patusan. In the middle of them walked a man dressed all in white. 'Look! It's him!' Cornelius cried. The group of people in the town stopped and looked up at the hill. Some pointed to the top of the hill, where Brown and his men were.

"Brown looked at his men. They were tired and hungry, and they didn't have much of a chance against so many people. He jumped up on the log to show the man in white that he wanted to talk. He held up his arms, palms out, to show that he was not carrying a gun.

"The man in white started walking toward the hill. Brown remained on the log until Jim reached the creek. Then, Brown jumped off the log and went down to meet him.

"They stood across the creek from each other, not far from where Jim took the second desperate leap of his life. That leap had landed him in the life of Patusan and its people. They might even have been on the exact spot where Jim had jumped. Each man gazed at the other with steady eyes, trying to understand what kind of man he was facing.

"Brown hated Jim at first sight. He was not the kind of man that Brown had expected to see. Whatever hopes Brown might have had about getting this outsider to help him take over Patusan vanished at once. That was enough reason for Brown to hate Jim.

"He also hated Jim because he was young and confident. He hated Jim's clear eyes and calm attitude. Jim had already gotten hold of this place, and he did not look like a man who needed anyone's help.

"He had all the advantages on his side. He owned the country, he had power, and he had all these people behind him. He was not hungry and desperate, and he did not seem afraid. Brown even hated Jim's neat appearance.

"'Who are you?' Jim asked at last, speaking very calmly.

"'My name is Brown,' the invader answered loudly. 'Captain Brown. What's yours?'

"'What made you come here?' Jim went on, as if he had not heard Brown's question.

"'Hunger. What made *you* come here?'

"'He jumped when I asked him that,' Brown told me. 'He jumped, and his face got red, as if he were too important to answer any questions. I told him that if he thought I was as good as dead, he wasn't any better off. I said I had a man up on the hill aiming a rifle at him, waiting for a signal from me to pull the trigger.

"'That didn't seem to bother him at all. "So let's agree," I said to him, "that we're both dead men. Let's talk as equals because we're all equal when it comes to dying." Then, I admitted that they had me like a rat in a trap, but I reminded him that even a trapped rat can bite.

"' "Not if you don't go near the trap till the rat is dead," he said.

"'I told him that I thought he was too good a man to let us all starve to death like that. I added that I wasn't going to beg for my life. "We're men, like you," I said to him, "and we're willing to die. However, if we have to die, we want to die fighting. So, come on and attack us, or let us go, and we'll take our chances starving on the open sea!

"' "You're one of us, even if you claim that you're with these people," I said. "What do they mean to you? What have you found here that's so precious? I'm not

a coward. Don't *you* be a coward. Come on and fight! Because we aren't going to starve up on that hill, and we aren't going into the forest to die one by one."

"'You don't deserve anything better,' Jim said.

"'What do *you* deserve?' Brown shouted back. 'You talk about your responsibility for these people and your duty! What do you know about me? I came here for food. What did *you* come for? All we're asking for is a good fight—or a clear road to go back where we came from.'

"'I'll fight with you now,' Jim offered.

"'I'd let you shoot me,' Brown said to Jim. 'This is as good a place as any to die. Still, that would be too easy. I have my men to think about. They're in the same position as me. I'm not the kind of man who jumps out of trouble and leaves my men behind.'

"'Jim stood thinking for a while,' Brown told me, 'and then wanted to know what I had done down the river. "Are we going to tell each other the story of our lives?" I asked him. "If we are, you begin."

"'But, he said nothing. "Oh, you don't want to tell me your story?" I said. "Well, keep it to yourself. I know it's no better than mine. I've done bad things. So did you—even if you talk like someone who should have wings, so you don't have to touch the dirty earth. Well, it *is* dirty, and I don't have wings.

"' "I'm here because I was afraid once in my life. Want to know what of? Prison. That scares me, and I don't mind telling you that it does. I won't ask what scared *you* and brought you to this place. You've done pretty well for yourself here. That's *your* good luck. My bad luck is to have to stand here and ask to be shot quickly or be kicked out to go free and starve."'

"Brown bent over in a coughing fit, as he lay on his miserable bed in that dirty hut. Then, he looked up at me, and his eyes gleamed with evil triumph. His thin body shook with a mad joy so powerful and so full of spite that it seemed to have driven off the death waiting for him.

"It's impossible to know how much Brown lied to Jim—how much he was lying to me then—and how much he lied to himself throughout his life. When he was through laughing, he continued his story.

"He admitted that Jim couldn't be scared. He told me with a crazy smile, 'I knew there was a way to get to him and shake his soul inside out!'

"Brown *did* figure out a way to get to Jim, but like everyone else, he never truly understood him. In the end, he did not turn Jim's soul inside out.

"To Jim, Brown's arrival in Patusan must have felt as though the world was playing a cruel joke on him. He had left the outside world. Now people from that world had invaded his refuge.[25]

"Yet, if he was being pursued by the outside world, why had it sent *these* men? Did *they* represent the world that he thought he wasn't good enough to live in? It's not surprising that Jim had very little to say to Brown.

"Brown was a devil. He had a gift for finding the weakest spot in his victims. He could see that Jim could not be won over with compliments. So, he talked about himself as a brave man who always had bad luck. As for coming to Patusan, how did these people know that he *didn't* come just to ask for food? They started shooting at him as soon as they saw him.

"The truth was that Dain Waris's quick attack had been the right thing to do, because it prevented terrible things from happening. Brown told me that, as soon as he saw how big Patusan was, and how many people lived there, he decided to set fire to the settlement and shoot every living thing he saw.

---

25. refuge a place that provides shelter or escape

That was the only way he'd be able to take over. Of course, he never told Jim this.

"He kept telling Jim a mix of truth and lies. The hardships Brown and his men had suffered were real. All Jim had to do was look at them. Brown whistled to his men, and they all stood up so Jim could see them. Brown admitted to Jim that they had killed the man in the village, but this was war, wasn't it? The Bugis had killed one of Brown's men, so they were even.

"Then, Brown said that surely Jim understood that when it came to saving your own life in the dark, a person didn't care how many other people died— 3, 30, or 300.

"'That made him jump!' Brown boasted to me. 'He just stood there, with nothing to say, looking at the ground.' Then, Brown asked Jim if there was nothing shameful in his own life, that he could be so hard on a man who was just trying to get out of a bad situation any way he could.

"All the while he talked to Jim, Brown kept referring to the things they had in common: their lives, their experience, their guilt—and a secret knowledge that there was a bond between them because they were very much alike.

"Finally, Brown stopped talking and waited to hear what Jim would say. At first, Jim didn't say anything. Along the river and from the houses in the town, hundreds of people stood watching in silence, waiting to see what Jim would decide.

"'Will you promise to leave?' Jim asked. Brown lifted his hand and let it fall to his side, indicating that he was willing to do whatever Jim wanted. 'Will you surrender your guns?' Jim added.

"'Surrender our guns? Not until you take them out of our dead hands. Do you think I'm crazy? My guns and the rags on my back are all I have in the world!'

"Jim was quiet again. Then, he said, as if speaking to himself, 'I don't know if I have the power...'

"'You don't know! Yet, you want me to give up my guns! What if they tell you that they'll do one thing and then do another thing to me? If you don't have the power, why are we talking to each other?'

"Jim stood in thought for a long time. Finally he said, 'Very well. You'll have a clear road, or you'll get your fight.' Then, he turned on his heel and walked away.

"Brown stood where he was, watching Jim until he disappeared among the houses in the settlement. He never saw Jim again.

"On his way back up the hill, Brown met Cornelius. 'Why didn't you kill him?' Cornelius demanded in a sour voice.

"'Because I can do better than that,' Brown answered, smiling.

"After this, events moved very fast. The rest of the story is seen through Tamb' Itam's eyes. Jim's faithful servant did not understand what happened any more than the others did. However, he remained completely loyal to Jim. As amazed as he was by what happened, he sadly accepted it as a mysterious failure that simply *had* to happen—because Tuan Jim allowed it to happen.

"Tamb' Itam's master returned from his meeting with Brown, went into one of the houses, and talked with Doramin. He remained alone with Doramin for a long time, and no one heard what they said to each other.

"Only Tamb' Itam, who stood close to the door, heard what his master said. 'Yes. I shall let all the people know that this is my wish. I speak to you, Doramin, before I speak to the others because you know my heart as well as I know your heart and your greatest desire. You know that I care only about what is good for the people of Patusan.'

"When Jim came out of the house, Tamb' Itam had a glimpse of old Doramin, sitting with his hands on his knees and looking down at his feet.

"Tamb' Itam followed his master to the fort where there was another meeting of the important people of the village. Tamb' Itam was hoping they would fight. 'It would be only taking another hill,' he told me sadly.

"Many other people in the town hoped that the invaders would simply leave, without a fight.

"Some of them felt that this was worse than the war with Sherif Ali. When that took place, many of them did not really care what happened. Now, everybody had something to lose. For the first time since Jim had come here, the people of Patusan did not agree with him.

" 'There was much talk, and at first my master was silent,' Tamb' Itam told me.

"Jim finally spoke. He said that these invaders were men who had suffered so much that they could no longer tell right from wrong. Lives had been lost, but why lose more? He reminded the people that their happiness was his happiness, their losses were his losses, and their grief was his grief.

"He reminded them that they had fought and worked side by side. They knew his courage, and they knew that he had never deceived them. For three years, they had lived together. Had he ever advised them badly? Had his words ever brought them suffering? He believed that it would be best to let these invaders leave.

"Jim told them that if the invaders were allowed to leave and any harm came to the people of Patusan as a result, he would answer with his own life. Then, Jim turned to Doramin. The old leader made no movement. This was his sign that he agreed with Jim.

"Jim trusted Brown enough to believe that he would leave Patusan. However, Jim did not understand to what lengths Brown would go to take revenge on anyone who resisted him. Jim was not aware of this, but he was worried that some mistake could cause fighting to break out.

"After the meeting, he told Jewel that he was going out of the fort to take command of the town. She did not want him to go, because he was tired and needed sleep. He said that he didn't want anything to happen for which he would never forgive himself.

"'I'm responsible for every life in the land,' he told her.

"'Are the men on the hill very bad?' Jewel asked.

"He thought before he answered. Then, he said, 'Men act badly sometimes, without being much worse than others.'

"When Jim left the fort, Tamb' Itam followed and remained close by his master, as Jim walked through the settlement to make sure that all was well. Tuan Jim gave his orders, and everyone obeyed him.

"When he finished with the town, Jim went to the Rajah's stockade. The old Rajah had fled to a small house that he owned near a jungle village.

"Kassim was in charge of the stockade. He was cool to Jim but said he was pleased when he was told that Jim and his men would take over the stockade for the night. The Rajah's stockade had a good view of the creek. It was the perfect place from which to watch Brown as he started down the river.

"Jim told Tamb' Itam to sleep, and the servant lay down on a mat near Jim. He could not sleep, though he knew he had an important mission later that night. Nearby, his master paced back and forth. Jim's head was bowed, his hands were behind his back, and his face was sad. At last, Jim came over to where Tamb' Itam lay and said softly, 'It is time.'

"Tamb' Itam's mission was to go down the river before Brown left and tell Dain Waris that the invaders were to be allowed to leave. Before he went, Tamb' Itam asked for something to prove that he was speaking words that came from Tuan Jim himself.

"Since arriving in Patusan, Jim had worn Stein's silver ring on his finger. Now, he took the ring off and gave it to Tamb' Itam.

"Jim had sent Brown a written message: 'You get the clear road. Start as soon as your boat floats on the morning tide. Let your men be careful. The bushes on both sides of the creek are full of well-armed men. You won't have a chance if there's a fight, but I don't believe you want more killing.'

"After Brown read Jim's message, he tore it into small pieces. Jim had chosen Cornelius to deliver the message because Brown knew Cornelius.

"Now, as Brown waited for the sun to come up so he and his men could leave this miserable place, Cornelius mumbled, 'You didn't kill him, and what have you gained? You could have had money from the Rajah. You could have stolen everything from all the Bugis houses. Now, you have nothing.'

"'You had better get out of here,' Brown growled without even looking at Cornelius.

"However, Cornelius began to whisper very fast, touching Brown's elbow from time to time. First, he told Brown about Dain Waris's armed men down the river. At first, Brown thought he had been betrayed, but then he decided that Jim would not do such a thing.

"Then, Cornelius mentioned that there was another way, a back way, down the river. He knew the river well, and he could show Brown this back way. That interested Brown. Next, Cornelius told Brown what had happened at the last meeting in town. 'So, he thinks he has made me harmless, does he?' mumbled Brown.

" 'Yes. He's a fool. A little child,' Cornelius hummed in Brown's ear. 'He came here and robbed me. He made all of the people believe him. If something happened that made them *not* believe him anymore, where would he be? Dain Waris, who is waiting for you down the river, is the very man who chased you up here when you came here.'

"Brown said quietly, as if he did not care, that it would be just as well to avoid Dain Waris.

"Cornelius answered quietly, as if *he* did not care, that the back way down the river would take Brown's boat past Dain Waris's camp. 'You'll have to be quiet,' he added, 'because we will pass right behind his camp.'

"Now, Brown was extremely interested. 'Oh, we know how to be very quiet, don't you worry.'

"Two hours before the sun came up, word was passed to the stockade that the invaders were going down to their boat. Soon, every armed man from one end of Patusan to the other was on the alert. Yet, the banks of the river remained so silent that it seemed as if the entire town was asleep.

"A thick, heavy mist lay low on the water, concealing everything. When Brown's boat glided out of the creek and into the river, Jim was standing in front of the Rajah's stockade—on the very spot where he first set foot on the Patusan shore. A shadow moved through the mist, and the murmur of low talking could be heard from Brown's boat.

"Brown sat with Cornelius next to him. They towed Cornelius's canoe behind the boat, so he would be able to return to Patusan later.

"When Jim spoke from the shore, Brown could hear him clearly. 'You have a clear road. Trust to the current while the fog lasts. The fog will lift soon.'

" 'Yes, soon we'll be able to see clearly,' replied Brown.

"Outside the stockade, the 30 or 40 men standing with their rifles ready held their breath.

"'When you reach your ship,' Jim told Brown, 'if you need to wait a day before heading out to sea, I'll send you some food.'

"'Yes. Do that,' came Brown's reply, muffled in the fog. Then, their boat floated away, fading, like a ghost, without the slightest sound.

"It was so foggy that the men in the boat could not even see the banks of the river.

"Cornelius began to whine about Jim, and Brown threatened to throw him out of the boat.

"'Throw me out, would you?' Cornelius mumbled. 'At least I'd know where I was. I've lived here long enough to see through a fog like this.'

"'Am I supposed to believe you could find that back way down the river in this fog?' Brown asked.

"'Of course I can! If you're not too tired to row.'

"'Out with your oars!' Brown shouted to his men.

"Cornelius showed the way, and for a long time, the boat crept through the fog in silence. There was nothing but dark gloom all around them, as if enormous wings were spread above the mist.

"Finally, Cornelius muttered something to Brown, and Brown ordered his men to load their rifles. 'I'll give you a chance to get even with them,' he said.

"Tamb' Itam had already arrived in Dain Waris's camp. When he approached the camp, two guards stepped out of the white mist to stop him. Then, other men appeared, and Tamb' Itam gave them the news. All was well. The trouble was over.

"When he entered the camp, Tamb' Itam demanded to be taken to Dain Waris.

"Jim's friend was still awake, lying on a bamboo platform covered with mats. Doramin's son greeted

Tamb' Itam warmly, and Tamb' Itam handed him the ring that proved he spoke for Jim.

"Leaning back on his elbow, Dain Waris listened to what Tamb' Itam had to say.

" 'The news is good. The invaders are leaving, with the consent of the village. They should be allowed to pass down the river.' Dain Waris toyed with Jim's ring as he listened and slipped it onto his finger.

"After Tamb' Itam reported what had happened at the last meeting, Dain Waris told him to eat some food and rest. Then, he gave orders to his men to prepare to return to Patusan that afternoon.

"Dain Waris lay down on his mat. Tamb' Itam talked to some men who wanted to hear what was happening in Patusan. The sun was eating up the mist. Dain Waris's men were watching the river where the invaders' boat was expected to appear at any moment. All was well in the camp.

"It was then that Brown took his revenge. Even as he lay on his deathbed, the memory of what he did gave him wicked, spiteful joy.

"His men landed quietly near the Bugis camp. Cornelius tried to sneak away, but Brown grabbed him and forced him to lead them to the camp. Holding both of Cornelius's skinny hands behind his back in the grip of one thick fist, Brown roughly shoved him forward as they sneaked up on the camp.

"At the edge of the forest, Brown's men spread themselves out under the trees and waited. They could see the entire camp, and no one knew they were there. Nobody had even dreamed that the invaders could have any knowledge of the back way down the river.

"When his men were ready, Brown yelled, 'Let them have it!' Thirteen shots rang out like one.

"The surprise in the camp was so great that no one moved at all after that first volley of shots.

Then, someone screamed, and yells of amazement and fear went up.

"In a blind panic, the Bugis ran up and down the shore of the river, like a herd of cattle afraid of the water. A few of them jumped into the river, but most didn't jump until after the last volley of shots.

"Brown's men fired three volleys into the camp. The entire time, Brown stood there, cursing and yelling, 'Aim low! Aim low!'

"Tamb' Itam understood what was happening as soon as the first shots were fired. Though he hadn't been hit, he fell down and lay still, as if he were dead. He kept his eyes open.

"At the sound of the first shots, Dain Waris, who was lying on his mat, jumped up and ran out into the open, where he was shot. Tamb' Itam saw him fling his arms wide open before he fell. At that moment, Tamb' Itam told me, a great fear came over him.

"The invaders vanished as they had come—unseen. For Brown, the slaughter was simply a lesson, a demonstration of some hidden and awful part of human nature.

"Brown had let Cornelius go before the shooting started. However, in the rush of getting away, Brown's men did not untie Cornelius's canoe. When they sped off in their boat, the canoe went with them.

"After the shooting stopped, Tamb' Itam rose from among the dead. He saw Cornelius running up and down the river, making little squeaking sounds. Suddenly, Cornelius rushed to the edge of the river and tried to take one of the Bugis' canoes. 'When he saw me coming,' Tamb' Itam told me, 'he threw himself on the ground, cried out, and began kicking at the air.'

"'What became of him?' I asked Tamb' Itam.

"Tamb' Itam made a stabbing gesture. 'I struck twice. He screeched like a frightened hen, and then he was still.'

"Many of Dain Waris's men survived the attack, but they were scattered and terrified. They did not know who had attacked them.

"For Tamb' Itam, the most important thing now was to be the first in Patusan with the awful news."

Chapter 15

"Paddling his canoe madly, Tamb' Itam returned to Patusan as fast as he could. When he arrived, he saw that the gate of the fort was wide open. People were standing on the shore of the river, waiting for the return of Dain Waris's boats. There was an air of celebration all through the settlement.

"Tamb' Itam jumped out of his canoe and ran toward Jim's house. The first person he met was Jewel.

"At first, Tamb' Itam stood before her without saying a word. His eyes were wild. Then, he started talking very quickly.

"'They have killed Dain Waris and many more men,' he told Jewel.

"She immediately ordered the gates of the fort to be shut. Jewel told Tamb' Itam to get Jim, and Tamb' Itam went into the house.

"As soon as he found Jim he cried out, 'Tuan, this is a day of evil, a day that has been cursed.' Jim raised himself on his elbow, just as Dain Waris had done, and Tamb' Itam began his story.

"He had not gotten very far when Jim sat up and said very quietly, 'Is Dain Waris dead?'

" 'It was a most cruel betrayal,' Tamb' Itam answered. 'Dain Waris ran out as soon as the first shots were fired, and he was killed.'

"Jim walked to the window and struck the shutter with his fist. Then, he began giving orders to assemble a fleet of boats to go after the invaders. Tamb' Itam didn't move.

"When Jim asked him why he was just standing there, Tamb' Itam said, 'Forgive me, Tuan, but...it is not safe for me to go out among the people.'

"Then Jim understood. He had retreated from one world because of a jump he had made without thinking. Now his other world, which he had built himself, had fallen in ruins around him. It was not safe for his servant to go out among his own people!

"I believe that was the moment when he decided to defy[26] the disaster in the only way that he thought he could.

"Without a word, he left his bedroom. He sat at the long table where the meetings had been held. He sat completely still, like a stone figure.

"Tamb' Itam had followed him and asked how he wanted the fort defended. Jim did not reply. Jewel came in and spoke to him, but he motioned with his hand that he did not want to talk. She went out on the porch and sat by the door, as if guarding him from the dangers outside.

"What was he thinking as he sat there? Everything was gone. He had once again lost everyone's confidence. I think it was then that he tried to write the letter that he never finished.

---

26. defy stand up to or face

"He remained there for a very long time. Toward evening, he called for Tamb' Itam and asked him what was going on in the settlement.

"Tamb' Itam said, 'There is much weeping and much anger. We shall have to fight.'

" 'Fight? What for?' Jim asked.

" 'For our lives.'

" 'I have no life,' Jim told Tamb' Itam.

" 'With enough courage and cunning we might be able to escape,' Tamb' Itam went on.

"Jewel came in, and Tamb' Itam left them alone. I don't have the heart to write down the little that she told me about that last time they were together. I will say that she spent an hour or more wrestling with him for her happiness.

" 'Fight!' she urged him. She could not understand that he felt there was nothing to fight for. He was going to prove his power in another way.

"Finally, he left the house and walked into the yard of the fort. Jewel followed him, breathless with fear and anger.

" 'Open the gates,' he ordered. Then, he told his men that they could return to their homes.

" 'For how long, Tuan?' asked one of them.

" 'For the rest of your life,' he said sadly.

"After the first cries of grief had swept over the river, a hush fell over the settlement. All kinds of rumors were flying everywhere. Some people said the invaders were coming back in a great ship, bringing many others with them. Some said there would be no place safe for anyone. Everyone was terrified.

"The sun was just going down when Dain Waris's body, covered with a white sheet, was laid at Doramin's feet. The old man sat stiffly for a long time, one hand on each knee, looking down. Before him stood all the Bugis, fully armed.

"When Doramin finally raised his eyes, he slowly looked over the crowd, as if seeking a missing face. Then, his chin sank onto his chest.

"After a while, Doramin gave a signal. The sheet was pulled back from Dain Waris's body. He looked as if he was asleep, and might awaken at any moment. Doramin leaned forward, his eyes searching the body from head to foot. He seemed to be looking for something. Perhaps for the wound.

"Someone standing next to the body took the silver ring from Dain Waris's cold, stiff hand and silently held it before Doramin. A murmur of shock and horror ran through the crowd.

"Doramin stared at the ring and let out a fierce cry from deep in his chest. It was a roar of pain and fury as mighty as the bellow of a wounded bull. The force of his anger and sorrow frightened everyone who heard that cry.

"Then, all was silent while the body was placed under a tree a short distance away. As the body was set down, all the women in Dain Waris's family began to wail.

"While this was happening, Jim was standing in the yard at the fort. Jewel stood in the doorway of the house, watching him. Tamb' Itam remained close by, waiting for Jim's orders.

"Jim turned his back on the house and on Jewel. He said to Tamb' Itam, 'It's time to finish this.'

"Tamb' Itam stepped forward, and Jewel walked into the yard. 'Will you fight?' she cried.

"'There is nothing to fight for,' he said.

"'Will you run?' she cried again.

"'There's no escape,' he said.

"'Then, you will go to Doramin?' she asked him. He nodded. 'Ah! You are insane, or you are a liar! Do you remember the night that I begged you to leave me, and you said that you could not? That it was impossible! You promised you would never leave me. You promised!'

"'If I ran away now,' he said, 'I would not be worth having.'

"'For the last time,' she cried desperately, 'will you defend yourself?'

"'Nothing can touch me,' he told her.

"At this, Jewel threw her arms round Jim and held him tightly. 'I will hold you here,' she sobbed. 'You are mine!' she cried on his shoulder.

"The sky over Patusan was blood-red, like an open vein. An enormous sun nestled bright red in the trees, and the forest had a black and forbidding face.

"Tamb' Itam saw Jim trying to unclasp Jewel's hands from around his neck. She clung to him so tightly that Jim could not free himself, and he called for Tamb' Itam to help him. With great difficulty, they got Jim free. He looked at Jewel, then ran to the river.

"Tamb' Itam followed Jim, and so did Jewel. After running only a few steps, she fell heavily to her knees.

"'Tuan! Tuan!' called Tamb' Itam. 'Look back!'

"Jim was already in a canoe, paddle in hand, and he did not look back. Tamb' Itam scrambled into the canoe just as it floated clear of the shore.

"As the canoe started up the river for Patusan, Jewel stood at the gate to the fort and screamed after Jim, 'You are false!'

"'Forgive me!' he cried.

"'Never! Never!' she called back.

"By the time they reached the settlement and approached Doramin's house, it was beginning to grow dark. Torches twinkled here and there. The people whom they met quickly stood aside to let Jim pass.

"When they arrived at Doramin's house, they heard women wailing. They saw that the yard was full of armed Bugis.

"Doramin sat in his chair, alone, immense, and sad beyond words. His two enormous, silver-trimmed pistols were on his knees. Before him stood the crowd of armed men.

"When Jim appeared, every head turned toward him. The crowd parted to let him through.

"When he stepped into the light of torches, the women stopped wailing. The night became silent. Doramin did not lift his head, and Jim stood before him without moving.

"Then, Jim slowly walked to Dain Waris's body, lifted the sheet, and looked at his dead friend. After a few seconds, he dropped the sheet without a word.

"As he walked back to Doramin, voices in the crowd murmured, 'He came! He came!' Someone said, 'He has taken it upon his own head.'

"Jim heard this and turned to the crowd. 'Yes. Upon my head.'

"Jim stood before Doramin for a short time. Then, Jim said quietly, 'I have come in sorrow.' When Doramin said nothing, he repeated, 'I have come, ready and unarmed.'

"The huge old man lowered his big forehead and made an effort to rise, clutching at the pistols on his knees. Two young men helped him to stand. From his throat came choking sounds that did not sound human.

"As he stood up, the silver ring, which was on his lap, fell and rolled against Jim's foot. Jim glanced down at the ring that had opened the door of fame, love, and success for him.

"Doramin swayed back and forth as he struggled to stay on his feet. He stared at Jim, his eyes full of enraged pain. Jim stood very still and looked straight at Doramin.

"Doramin slowly raised his right hand and shot his son's friend. Jim glanced at the people on his right and on his left, with a look that was proud and steady. Then, he fell forward, dead.

"Impossible to understand, he passes away under a cloud—a romantic to the very end. Not in the wildest dreams of his childhood could he have imagined such a success!

"For it may very well be that, in the short moment of his last proud and steady glance, he saw the face of that *opportunity*, which had finally come to him.

"He is gone, and Jewel is leading a quiet life in Stein's house. Stein has aged greatly. He says that he is 'preparing to leave all this,' while he waves his hand sadly at his butterflies."

September 1899–July 1900

REVIEWING YOUR READING

CHAPTER 1 (PAGES 1–5)

FINDING THE MAIN IDEA

1. Which of the following best states the main idea of this chapter?

    (A) A ship's chandler sells goods to sailors. (B) Jim was born in England. (C) Jim is a sailor with a mysterious past. (D) The *Patna* was an old steamer with a German captain.

REMEMBERING DETAILS

2. On the training ship, Jim does not immediately get into the rescue boat because

    (A) he is in awe of the storm. (B) he is lazy. (C) he does not want to take part in the rescue. (D) there is not enough room in the lifeboat.

DRAWING CONCLUSIONS

3. In the first chapter, Conrad is suggesting that

    (A) Jim will never be prepared to meet any danger as long as he is living a life at sea. (B) Jim should not have become a sailor. (C) Jim later decides he does not want a life at sea because it is too dangerous. (D) Jim dreams about a life of adventure but is not prepared for how dangerous life at sea can be.

IDENTIFYING THE MOOD

4. When Conrad writes about Jim as a young man, the mood is

    (A) exciting and reckless. (B) confident and hopeful. (C) confident and sad. (D) angry and dangerous.

CRITICAL THINKING

5. **Inference** Why do you think Jim was popular in the eastern ports where he worked as a water-clerk?

6. **Comprehension** In the first chapter, Conrad writes that Jim had another name, but he does not want anyone to know it. Why does he keep this a secret?

7. **Analysis** When Jim is injured on his first job as a sailor, he has to remain in his cabin during the storm. Why do you think he is glad he does not have to be on deck?

CHAPTERS 2–4 (PAGES 5–25)

FINDING THE MAIN IDEA

1. What is the main event that takes place in these chapters?

   (A) Jim becomes angry with Marlow because of what he hears. (B) Marlow decides to stop going to the trial. (C) Jim's trial ends. (D) We learn what happened aboard the *Patna*.

REMEMBERING DETAILS

2. Jim becomes angry with Marlow outside the courtroom because

   (A) Marlow was staring at him during the trial.
   (B) he thinks Marlow has called him a miserable dog.
   (C) he does not want to be on trial. (D) Marlow refuses to give Jim a job on his ship.

DRAWING CONCLUSIONS

3. On the *Patna*, the second engineer falls down because

   (A) he is seasick and has lost his balance. (B) the captain has hit him. (C) the ship has run over something in the water. (D) he is trying to run away.

IDENTIFYING THE MOOD

4. The mood at the beginning of Chapter 2 is

    (A) peaceful. (B) tense. (C) sad. (D) excited.

CRITICAL THINKING

5. **Analysis** When the crew thinks the ship is sinking, how are Jim's actions the same or different from the other crew members of the *Patna*? Explain you answer.

6. **Evaluation** Why do you think the harbor master calls the captain of the *Patna* a hound?

7. **Inference** Jim becomes angry when he thinks he has been called a miserable dog. What does this say about Jim?

CHAPTERS 5–6 (PAGES 26–38)

FINDING THE MAIN IDEA

1. The main point of Marlow's conversation with Chester is that

    (A) Chester has a lot of respect for Jim. (B) Marlow does not want to help Jim find work. (C) now that the trial is over, Jim will be offered good jobs. (D) people think that Jim will now take jobs nobody else wants.

REMEMBERING DETAILS

2. The men in the lifeboat thought that the *Patna* had sunk because

    (A) they could not see the *Patna's* lights.
    (B) they heard shouts coming from the *Patna*.
    (C) the captain told them he saw the *Patna* sink.
    (D) they saw people jumping off the ship.

DRAWING CONCLUSIONS

3. When Jim leaves the balcony of Marlow's hotel room,

    (A) he feels his life has been ruined. (B) he has decided to go into the shipping business. (C) he is more hopeful about his future. (D) he plans to go back to England and make a new life for himself.

UNDERSTANDING CHARACTER

4. Marlow offers money to Jim so he can leave town, but Jim refuses. What does this tell you about Jim's character?
   (A) He is foolish. (B) He is honorable. (C) He is cowardly. (D) He is untrustworthy.

CRITICAL THINKING

5. **Analysis** Why do you think Conrad includes Marlow's conversation with the French naval officer? What ideas are conveyed in this part of the novel?
6. **Evaluation** What does Jim mean when he says to Marlow, "There wasn't the thickness of a sheet of paper between the right and wrong of this whole business"?
7. **Comprehension** Why is it so important to Jim that he stand trial and not run away?

CHAPTERS 7–8 (PAGES 39–47)

FINDING THE MAIN IDEA

1. The main point in these chapters is that
   (A) Jim is dishonest. (B) Jim is a troublemaker with a hot temper. (C) Jim is a romantic who has let many opportunities slip by. (D) Jim does not care about what any other people think.

REMEMBERING DETAILS

2. What did Jim do to the Danish officer who insulted him?
   (A) He beat him with his fists. (B) He bought a meal for him and befriended him. (C) He threw him off a balcony. (D) He told him the true story of what had happened to him.

DRAWING CONCLUSIONS

3. Jim quits his job at Egstrom & Blake because
   (A) he does not like the job anymore. (B) someone from the *Patna* threatened to tell Jim's secret. (C) Blake thinks he is doing a bad job. (D) Egstrom does not want to pay him as much money as he is worth.

MAKING INFERENCES

4. Schomberg, the Bangkok hotel owner, knew Jim's secret, but he still liked him. However, after Jim got into a fight Schomberg said, "A man with a temper like that can't stay here." What can you infer from this?

(A) Schomberg just wanted an excuse to fire Jim.
(B) Schomberg is a business man who cares more about his hotel than about Jim. (C) Schomberg does not care what happens in the hotel.(D) Schomberg will try to convince Jim to stay.

CRITICAL THINKING

5. **Application** In Chapter 7, Marlow wonders if Jim is facing the ghost that haunts him or is running away from it. What ghost is haunting Jim?

6. **Evaluation** Compare how Stein responds to his opportunity with the butterfly with how Jim responds to his opportunity on the *Patna*.

7. **Comprehension** What does Stein mean when he says about Jim, "He is a romantic"?

CHAPTERS 9–12 (PAGES 47–78)

FINDING THE MAIN IDEA

1. The main thing that happens in these chapters is that

(A) Jim decides to go to sea and finds work on a ship.
(B) Jim goes to Patusan and begins his life anew.
(C) Jim becomes shipwrecked on a jungle island.
(D) Jim gives up his dreams of becoming an honorable man.

REMEMBERING DETAILS

2. The three most powerful people in Patusan are

(A) Doramin, the Rajah, and Sherif Ali. (B) Doramin, the Rajah, and Cornelius. (C) Doramin, the Rajah, and Jewel. (D) Dain Waris, Tamb' Itam, and Marlow.

MAKING INFERENCES

3. You can infer that the night Jim is to be killed by Sherif Ali's men, the signal to kill him was to be given by (A) Doramin. (B) Sherif Ali. (C) Jewel. (D) Cornelius.

IDENTIFYING THE MOOD

4. The night Jim faces the men in the storehouse, the mood is (A) romantic. (B) happy. (C) tense. (D) sad.

CRITICAL THINKING

5. **Application** If Jewel and Cornelius were creatures in Stein's insect collection, what do you think they would be?
6. **Evaluation** Why do you think Jim calls the woman he loves "Jewel"? Explain you answer.
7. **Comprehension** Explain why Stein gave Jim the silver ring.

CHAPTERS 13–15 (PAGES 78–113)

FINDING THE MAIN IDEA

1. The main thing that is revealed in Chapter 13 is that

   (A) Brown and his crew go to Patusan, where they plan to take over. (B) Marlow stays to fight Brown. (C) Marlow meets Brown. (D) Brown and his men steal a ship and flee across the open sea.

REMEMBERING DETAILS

2. Brown and his men are able to surprise Dain Waris's camp because

   (A) there is a thick mist over the river. (B) Kassim lies to Dain Waris. (C) Dain Waris' guards were asleep. (D) Cornelius shows them a back way down the river.

DRAWING CONCLUSIONS

3. At the meeting of village leaders, Doramin does not agree to attack Brown because

    (A) he thinks that it was useless to fight Brown.
    (B) he knows Jim will be back soon. (C) he thinks Brown will leave without a fight. (D) he fears that his son will die in battle.

CHARACTER MOTIVATION

4. Why does Jim agree to let Brown leave?

    (A) He is afraid that Brown will win if they actually fight.
    (B) He is thinking of Jewel and is concerned for her safety.
    (C) He is thinking of how he once acted himself and is giving Brown another chance. (D) He realizes that Brown does not have the will to fight.

CRITICAL THINKING

5. **Comprehension** At the beginning of Chapter 13, Conrad changes the time and place of the story. What is this change?

6. **Analysis** Why do you think Brown hates Jim at first sight?

7. **Evaluation** Do you think Jewel is right not to forgive Jim? Explain your answer.